LOVE, UNDISCLOSED

MAX LOUISE PERRY

Cover Design by Rena Violet

ISBN: 978-1-8384046-0-4 (paperback)

www.maxlouiseperry.com

For Devin, for always listening.

ONE

Sweat stuck Julienne's bangs to her forehead as she pedalled away on the stationary bike. She could hear someone having an argument with her personal trainer in the corner of the gym, but she resisted the urge to turn off the electronic music pumping through her headphones and eavesdrop.

She watched, instead, in the reflection in the windows as the woman with the familiar shock of curly blonde hair gestured wildly. She knew most of the gym regulars, and Cece was no exception.

Julienne spent hours at the gym every week, and all the regulars of the gym formed a steady backdrop to her life. It was a nice place to people watch when her life felt empty, and so different from the gym at UCLA, where she always bumped into someone she knew.

For a moment, Julienne could forget all her worries. There were many, and they seemed to be multiplying by the day; the unread email from her parents haunting her inbox, the job interview she still hadn't heard back from.

She steadily reduced the resistance on the bike, stretched, and headed to the locker room. She had a favourite locker, one she tried to use every time. It felt a little silly, but she'd always been a creature of habit, following the same gym routine through her whole time on the college tennis team.

She tugged at the door, remembering the catch when the locker had jammed a few days ago. That was when she'd learnt Cece's name, wearing only a towel, her hair dripping wet around her shoulders, swearing at her locker.

Cece had appeared, as if by magic, and given her a beaming smile and jiggled the key in just the right way. The locker had opened under her skilled hands, and Julienne had flushed and thanked her profusely.

"Easy," Cece had said. "We should pretend it was harder, though, because I'm hiding from my trainer."

Julienne had just blinked at her, still clutching her towel to her chest. "You're not here by choice?" she'd asked.

Cece had laughed. "You're one of those masochists, then, who actually enjoys time at the gym?"

"Pretty much," Julienne had said. She'd been thrown off by Cece's easy confidence, her willingness to invade Julienne's space, even if it was to help her out. "I'm here because it makes me happy. You should do what makes you happy."

Cece had given her a wry smile, then, as if she was considering Julienne. "It's definitely not that simple," she'd said, eventually. Then: "I'm Cece, by the way."

Julienne had introduced herself in turn. It had been nice to put a name to the face – she'd seen Cece around chatting to the staff and some of the other regulars, and she'd wondered why this woman was always trailed by an exasperated personal trainer. She wasn't sure she had any answers yet.

She shook herself. She'd had so little social interaction lately that just a brief conversation seemed to stand out.

Tonight was important, and she couldn't afford to get distracted. Her best friend Reina was in town, for the first time in months. She needed to shower quickly so she could get home and get ready.

Soon, Julienne smelled like her favourite shampoo, and she let the changing room door swing shut behind her, running a towel through her hair one last time. There was a woman Julienne didn't recognise at the reception desk, wearing a dress and a smart jacket, leaning against the counter and watching her. Julienne tucked her towel into her bag.

"Julienne?" The woman pushed off the counter and stood up straight, pasting on a smile.

Julienne blinked. "That's me," she said warily.

"Can I walk you to your car?"

Julienne glanced at the receptionist, who was studying her computer screen with unusual ferocity.

"I walked here," Julienne said. "Can I help you?"

"My name is Sadie Cole," the woman said. "I work with another member of the gym. I was here to meet with her and she suggested I talk to you. Do you have a moment to talk about a job opportunity?"

Julienne raised her eyebrows. She thought of the interview she'd had the other day, the long pause in conversation when her friends asked what she'd been up to and she'd had to tell them 'nothing'.

"What kind of job?"

Sadie pursed her lips. "I'm not at liberty to say right now."

Julienne frowned. "No offense," she said, "but this sounds like a scam."

"It's not a sales job or anything," Sadie said quickly. "It will involve forming a personal relationship with my client."

That did nothing to ease Julienne's worries. "Like an escort?" she said.

Julienne hoped she hadn't been picked out as the only member of the gym who was obviously unemployed. It was expensive, sure, but she'd paid for six months up front and she had a plan. She had goals. Escorting didn't fit in with that.

"No," Sadie said. She paused. "I could provide more details if you sign a non-disclosure agreement."

"Thank you for your interest," Julienne said, taking a step back from Sadie. She was sure the woman noticed. "It doesn't sound like something I'm looking for right now."

Sadie's brow furrowed. "I understand," she said. Another awkward pause. "Here, take my card in case you change your mind. I promise you, it's all above board."

Julienne took the card and shoved it in her back pocket, certain she would never call it.

"Thanks, anyway," Julienne said. Sadie nodded, and Julienne took that as permission to leave, hurrying out the door of the gym into the fresh air.

She put it out of her mind as she walked home. The entrance of her apartment building was a nice reprieve from the LA heat, and her damp hair was heavy on her shoulders as she climbed the dimly lit stairs. She said hi to her roommate, Tori, and warmed up some leftovers before disappearing into her room to get ready.

When Julienne had plans to feel excited about and structure to her day, she could almost believe that she was living her dream in LA. She was so in love with the idea of it, living in the city she loved, a college friend as a roommate, working in an art gallery.

She'd been here for 4 years, attending college, and it felt more like her home than her old life in England.

She brushed out her long brown hair and blow dried it, letting it settle around her shoulders, and used some hairspray to keep her bangs in the right place. She slicked a line of glittery eyeshadow above both her eyes, the gold a pleasant contrast to her blue eyes. Julienne couldn't remember the last time she'd worn make up, but she wanted to dress up. She put on some clear lipgloss as a finishing touch, and then put on the clothes she'd picked out earlier – a print button down that she'd cut to be cropped and a denim skirt. She removed the elastic hair tie from her wrist and replaced it with a plain silver bangle. She considered herself in the mirror and wondered if her already fair skin was a little paler than usual from all the time spent indoors.

"You ready?" Tori asked, leaning on the doorway to her bedroom. She was the tallest member of the tennis squad and made for a striking figure in the doorway, her purple sequined dress seeming to sparkle in the light. She'd loosely curled her jaw-length brown hair and she wore a bold red lipstick. The blush on her cheeks warmed up her fair skin.

"I need to find my shoes," Julienne said, looking around her room. It was usually immaculate but she'd gotten sloppy the longer she'd been unemployed.

"There's a pair of yours by the front door," Tori said, smiling. "The black brogues?"

"Probably left them there last time we went out," Julienne said. She rarely had occasion to wear shoes other than trainers.

"When we ditched early, you mean." Tori smirked at her.

"Oh god," Julienne groaned. "We're the flaky friends. I bet Aubrey hates us for it."

"Aubrey should stop inviting us to parties when they

know we'll leave early," Tori said. "If we set a date to play tennis together with everyone we'd stay the whole time."

"Have you met us? We'd get way too competitive."

Tori laughed. "Plus, we'd be missing Reina. Who would you partner with?"

"I don't think I can match up to Reina anymore. She's a pro now. She'd wipe the floor with us."

"With me, maybe," Tori said. "You're always at the gym, working out."

"You've just got better things to do than go to the gym," Julienne shot back.

She grabbed her handbag and switched out the light, stopping in the hallway to put on her boots.

"The queer journalist network is putting on a lot of events," Tori said. "It keeps me busy."

They chatted about their days as Tori locked up their apartment door and they waited for the Uber. The emptiness of unemployment had meant Julienne had withdrawn from all her friendships, and she regretted it as soon as she had a normal conversation with Tori. It was easy to forget there was a world outside staring at her email inbox and going to the gym.

They weren't meeting everyone on the team tonight, just their little group that had formed in freshman year. Reina had got them all together then, and she'd done the same now; she was the natural leader of the group and her charisma outshone them all. Julienne felt lucky to be along for the ride, tagged in by being assigned Reina's roommate the first time the team traveled together. Even though they'd been a solid group ever since, it had always felt like they were more Reina's friends than Julienne's. She was on the periphery, and always felt weird about initiating an invite to something if Reina wasn't there.

They thanked the Uber driver and Tori swiped through to give him five stars as they stood outside the bar. They were a little late to arrive, but this bar, the same one they'd frequented as students, made Julienne's fondness for strict timekeeping disappear. Reina had chosen the venue out of nostalgia and nobody wanted to overrule her when it was the first time they'd seen her in months.

They opened the door to high pitched squeals from the corner booth and moments later Julienne was wrapped in hugs from the four people waiting for them. Last was Reina, who grinned at her before giving her a warm, tight hug.

It had been too long.

TWO

"Drinks, we need drinks," Mia said, as Julienne stepped back from Reina's embrace. She kept their arms linked, relishing the contact.

Reina grinned. "A round of shots, to start?"

Aubrey and Mia cheered in response and Julienne couldn't help but laugh.

"It's on me," Reina said, and disappeared to the bar.

Julienne squeezed into the booth beside the others, finding herself beside Aubrey, her forearms pressed against the sticky table. She tried not to feel claustrophobic. Reina returned carrying a tray of tequila shots, slices of lime haphazardly placed on the tray along with a lone salt shaker. She placed it on the table, grinning, and then slid in next to Tori.

"Two each," she announced, picking two glasses up. "It's our big reunion."

"You're a bad influence," Tori groaned, but moved two glasses closer to her.

Julienne followed suit. "Athletics suits you," she said to Reina.

Reina blew her a kiss. "Work hard, play hard," she said.

Julienne couldn't stop grinning. It was so good to feel like she was back in it again, part of the group. Reina's presence helped, her unshakeable confidence rubbing off on Julienne, but she was also realizing that she and Tori were the only two who hadn't pregamed for this, and everyone else being a little drunk helped too.

Mia started talking, detailing their itinerary for the evening. Julienne felt tired just listening to her enthusiasm. Things had gotten wild in Junior year when they'd all finally turned 21, but since then she'd slowed down a little. She missed the illicit thrill of drinking under age, the bonfires and house parties where she could linger on the edges, only get as involved as she wanted to.

"I have to pee," Aubrey announced, bringing Julienne back to the present. There was some shuffling as Reina moved to let them and Mia out of the booth, and then the two of them disappeared to the bathroom.

"You okay?" Reina asked, sliding back into the booth and nudging Julienne softly with her elbow.

Julienne shrugged. "Happy to see you, Ray. Are you having a good night?"

"It's only the start of the night," Reina said. "I want you to have fun too, babe."

"That's code for you bullying me into karaoke later, isn't it?" Julienne said.

"You'll enjoy it and you know you will," Reina said. "But that's now what's important right now."

Julienne raised her eyebrows.

"How have you been?" Reina said, drawing out the last word. Her eyeshadow glittered as her eyes fluttered dramatically, and in the lighting of the bar her brown skin seemed to glow.

Julienne made eye contact with Tori, silently commiserating about how boring both their lives were compared to Reina's jetsetting to competitions. "I'm doing okay," she told Reina honestly. "Not much to say, it's just kind of the same thing every week."

"Job hunt?" Reina asked, looking sympathetic. Julienne tried not to resent that Reina had just skipped that whole stressful part of graduate life.

"Lots of rejections," Julienne said. "I had an interview the other day, though."

"Rejection sucks," Reina said, and Tori made a sympathetic noise on Julienne's other side.

"Eventually someone's going to say yes," Julienne said.

Reina nodded, her hand reaching beneath the table to squeeze Julienne's. "Just need to have faith," she said.

"Definitely," Tori agreed.

"How about you?" Julienne asked, eager to change the subject. "How's the tennis going?"

Reina rolled her eyes and launched into one of her stories, vivacious as always, complaining about her personal trainer's specific diet requirements. All the while, though, she kept their hands together under the table, and the point of contact made Julienne feel like maybe she could let go of the stress of jobhunting for a night.

It was so easy to slip back into how it had always been and joke around and forget that actually, they'd all graduated college and were living different lives now. All of them squeezed into one too-small booth, a little drunk and silly. Aubrey's stories were still outrageous – they'd somehow ended up at a party on a yacht when they were scared of the sea – and Mia was still their partner in crime, and Reina was still perfectly Ray and everything was the same. Tori was the group's anchor, tall and quiet in the corner, and Julienne felt like she was a part of something again.

They ordered another round of drinks and Julienne felt the night beginning to blur at the edges. Time seemed to speed up after that, and soon they were moving to another bar. Music videos were playing on the tv screen behind the bar, and Reina was in the middle of poking her in the ribs when she thought she saw someone she recognised.

"You're totally staring," Aubrey giggled, and Julienne was grateful she wasn't the drunkest in the room.

"I know her!" Julienne said. "The girl in the video, she's called Cece, she goes to my gym."

She looked different all made up, a serious look on her face.

"Wait, Cece?" Mia said, suddenly alert and leaning towards Julienne with an intense expression on her face. "Cece Browne? I'm obsessed with Bare Windows, the first season was so good."

"She's an actress?" Julienne asked. She'd seemed so down-to-earth, Julienne hadn't realised she was a celebrity.

Mia nodded, her eyes lit up in a way Julienne hadn't seen since Junior year. Reina laughed softly.

"Have you talked to her?" Mia said.

Julienne laughed. "We had a two-minute conversation. I've noticed her around, though."

"I bet you have," said Reina, her voice thick with innuendo.

Julienne rolled her eyes. "She argues with her trainer."

Tori wrinkled her nose. "That sounds pleasant."

Julienne shrugged.

"I can't believe you go to a gym with celebrities," Reina said. "You must have some stories."

Julienne grimaced. "Not really," she said. "Someone

offered me a shady sounding job when I left today, something about forming a personal relationship with their client."

"Hooker!" Aubrey said, loudly enough that someone at the next table turned and looked.

"Don't call them that," Tori said.

There was a beat of silence. "I asked if it was escorting and she said no," Julienne offered.

Reina's eye's sparkled. "You should do it."

"No way," Julienne said. Reina didn't have *that* much sway over her.

"I dare you." Reina was grinning, all teeth and gums.

"Me too!" Aubrey said, bouncing in their chair a little. "I always wanted a friend who-" they paused, glancing at Tori.

Tori shook her head and Aubrey's cheeks turned a little pink.

Julienne tried not to laugh at the exchange. "I think the right term is sex work," she told Aubrey. "I'm not going to do it, though, who knows what it could be?"

"What if Cece Browne needs a new personal trainer?" Mia said. "You could get her to come to drinks with us!"

"I'm not calling her," Julienne said, but she could feel herself grinning, her resolve weakening. It was hard, when they all ganged up on her.

"She gave you her number?" Aubrey said, leaning in.

Mia shrieked and made grabby hands. "I have so many questions about season two! You have to call her!"

"It's not her number," Julienne said, laughing and shaking her head. The bright lights of the bar seemed to shimmer a little and she was starting to regret the last drink she'd had. "The woman at the gym. She just gave me her card."

"C'mon Julienne," Reina said. "It's just a phone call."

Julienne met Reina's eyes. Reina, whose smile seemed more knowing than anybody else was capable of. She could think of half a dozen times Reina had talked her into something at college, and it only sometimes ended badly.

She caved. "I'll call her tomorrow," she said, and the whole table broke out in cheers.

"We need another round to celebrate," Reina declared, standing up. Julienne blinked at her, silhouetted in the bright lights. She was pretty sure another round was the last thing she needed.

Tori laughed. "I think you're the only one of us who'll still get served here."

"Athlete's constitution," Reina said. "One round, then we go to a club and we dance."

Mia groaned. "But people are pretty here and I haven't got anyone's number yet."

Julienne laughed. "There will be other pretty people," she said.

Mia pouted. Reina went to the bar, and the rest of the group turned to planning Mia's next move on the guy she had her eye on.

The next drink went down easily, and then there was another and another and a dance floor and a blur of bright lights and heavy bass.

She didn't remember much of the ride home, but she remembered the smile on her face.

THREE

Her alarm went off too early. It was exactly the same time as usual, but her head was pounding and her throat felt dry. She took a sip of water and ran her tongue over her teeth. They felt gummy, grimy, even though she vividly remembered determinedly brushing her teeth before she went to bed.

She brushed her teeth and showered, keeping an eye on the clock. She put some concealer on to cover up the dark circles beneath her eyes, and tried not to notice how pale she was. It was a permanent reminder that she didn't get out much.

She was fifteen minutes early to meet Reina at the mall, so she lingered in her car, scrolling mindlessly on her phone. Reina was rarely early, and she wasn't sure she was ready to face a crowd alone just yet.

Her phone started ringing as she was looking at it – an unknown number. The potential it held made her heart skip a beat. It could be a job offer, or a scammer, or just Reina calling to say she was late.

Her hand was a little sweaty as she pressed on her

phone screen to answer it.

"Hello," she said.

"Hi, is this Julienne Taylor?"

"Speaking."

"It's Madison, from the Carter Gallery. We met the other day."

Julienne blinked and sat up a little straighter, hoping she sounded more alert than she felt. "It's great to hear from you," she said. This was it. Her dream job, almost in her grasp. Carter Gallery was one of her favourites, and she thought the interview had gone well.

Hope put her heart in her throat.

"We've decided to go with another candidate," Madison said, a little bluntly.

Julienne swallowed, feeling the heavy stone of disappointment sinking in her gut. She took a moment to find the words to react. "Oh," She said. She was glad it was just a phone call, and Madison couldn't see that she was tearing up. "Thank you for letting me know. Would you be able to provide any feedback on my interview?"

"You just didn't stand out," Madison said. "Good luck with the job search."

She hung up, and Julienne was left staring at her blank phone screen, a lump forming in her throat.

She'd really thought she had a chance of getting that job, of starting down the path to her dream. She didn't even know what she was doing wrong. It was the third interview she'd had a flat rejection from, with no real feedback.

She was losing count of the rejections she'd had overall. It was starting to feel like nobody was going to take a chance on her.

She swallowed and swiped through to her emails. The email from her parents still sat at the top of her inbox, unopened, but there was no better time to rip-off the band-aid. She already felt like shit. It was hard to see it getting much worse.

She wished she'd bought herself a coffee before doing this.

"Babe!" Reina said, tapping on the window of her car. Julienne looked up from her phone. "Oh no, are you okay?"

At least she never needed to put up a front with Reina. She grabbed her handbag and waited for Reina to step back so she could open the door.

"Let's get some coffee," she said. "The last interview just called to reject me, and my parents are going to stop paying my rent."

Reina whistled. "That blows. I'm so sorry."

Reina pulled her into a hug, and Julienne tried to relax and let go of the stress. Reina had always been her biggest cheerleader, at whatever she was trying to do. It was a relief that she wasn't facing this alone in her apartment.

"It's fine," she said. "I knew it was coming, I'd have to go home eventually."

"Are you sure you don't want something stronger than coffee?"

Julienne rolled her eyes. "It's 10am and I have a hang-over," she said.

Reina shrugged. "I'll buy your coffee, anyways. Come on."

Reina linked her arm through Julienne's and steered her towards the entrance of the mall.

The lump in Julienne's throat seemed to grow as Reina took charge, leading the way to the coffee place and pushing Julienne towards a plush armchair.

"Same order as usual?" Reina asked.

Julienne nodded.

Reina gave her a quick, reassuring smile and joined the queue at the counter.

She hadn't been home in years. She wasn't ready to leave LA.

If she moved back to England, who knew when she'd see Reina, or Tori, or anyone else again. England was the other side of the world; it wasn't like they could just drop in for a weekend.

It wasn't like she had much of a choice anyway.

Reina returned before she had a chance to spiral any more, and placed a cup of coffee and a cupcake in front of her.

"It's not the end of the world," Reina said. "We have cupcakes!"

"Is this on your trainer's diet?"

Reina winked at her, and Julienne couldn't help but laugh.

Reina tucked her dark hair behind her ears, looking earnest. "I have an idea for how to cheer you up," she said.

Julienne raised an eyebrow.

"Call that number you got yesterday," Reina said. "Ask about the job. It could be the opportunity of a lifetime."

"It could be nothing, or worse than nothing," Julienne said.

"The only way to find out is to call her," Reina said pointedly. "You promised you would last night."

"You're mean," Julienne said.

Reina grinned at her.

"Can we at least google the company first?" Julienne asked.

Reina conceded and Julienne fished the business card out of her pocket. It already looked a little worse for wear. The two of them huddled around Julienne's phone as she typed in the name of the company – Harper & Perez Management – into google, and clicked through to their website.

It was hard not to feel nostalgic for all the other times she and Reina had ended up doing a post-mortem of their night out, scrolling through social media with bleary eyes to find out something about someone from the night before. It was how Reina had met her boyfriend in junior year, and Julienne had used it to put a name to the face of someone she had a crush on more than once.

She took a sip of her coffee and passed her phone to Reina, who was clearly more invested in this than she was.

"They manage celebrities," Reina said, lifting her head up, her dark eyes meeting Julienne's. "They do PR, too. It doesn't look like a scam at all."

"Do they have a list of clients?" Julienne asked.

Reina shook her head. "Their website is slick and professional. Looks expensive."

"You would know," Julienne said.

Reina smirked at her. "Stop delaying. Call them."

Julienne swallowed. "Fine," she said, tapping the number into her phone, trying to channel Reina's cool confidence.

It only rang twice.

"Sadie Cole," a crisp voice answered. Reina leaned forward, trying to listen in.

Julienne tried to conjure up her professional phone manner. "It's Julienne Taylor, you gave me your card yesterday?"

There was a brief pause and both Julienne and Reina were holding their breath. "Of course," Sadie said. "You've changed your mind?"

"I'd like to know more," Julienne said, choosing her words carefully.

"I work for Harper & Perez Management," Sadie said. "Are you available this afternoon? We could discuss it in person, but I'll need to see your résumé and you'll need to sign a non-disclosure agreement."

"I'm available," Julienne said. Reina nodded encouragingly. "Any time after two?"

Sadie read out the address, which led to a sudden scramble for the notebook and pen that Julienne kept in her handbag, but soon Julienne had an appointment at an address closer to Hollywood than she'd ever needed to venture. She hung up, feeling a little breathless. She was glad, at least, that her emergency notebook finally had a use.

Reina grinned at her. "Did I hear the words non-disclosure agreement?"

"If I get kidnapped I'm holding you responsible," Julienne said.

Reina rolled her eyes. "It's going to be fine," she said.

Julienne took another sip of her coffee. "I should go home and get changed," she said.

"You've been recruited," Reina said, "you don't have to impress anyone."

"That's definitely not true."

"I thought you didn't even want this job," Reina said, smirking.

"I always like to make a good impression," Julienne said, not meeting Reina's eyes. The feedback from the last interview replayed in her head. She needed to stand out.

She didn't know how to stand out to someone who dealt with celebrities on a daily basis.

Reina rolled her eyes. "Finish your coffee and we'll go back to yours, get you all prettied up."

Julienne nodded, gave her a small smile. "Thanks for cheering me up," she said.

Reina shrugged, smiling back at her. "I've missed this."

"In college you were usually the one with the crisis," Julienne said.

Reina laughed. "Yeah, I needed you to keep me in line," she said.

They dawdled over their coffees, reminiscing about college. It was a pleasant way to spend an hour, and Julienne felt herself relaxing the more time she spent with Reina.

They drove separately back to Julienne's place, Reina somehow managing to beat her there in the flashy rental car she was driving. As they climbed the stairs Reina mused aloud about what outfit Julienne should wear, as though they were still living in each other's pockets and knew every inch of each other's wardrobes. For the first time, Julienne wondered if Reina was as lonely as she was when they were apart.

"I miss living with you," Reina said, looking around the apartment. Tori wasn't in but you could see her mark on the place, the spice rack in the kitchen and the cushion embroidered with the trans flag. An art print that had lived in Julienne's dorm room was now framed and hanging on the wall, and there were some photos of the whole tennis team in a frame on the bookshelf.

They only got a little bit sidetracked before Reina was rooting through Julienne's wardrobe with considerable enthusiasm. Julienne didn't want to wear the same outfit she'd worn for the last interview. It felt tainted, now, so when Reina pulled out the shirt she'd worn she shook her head and put it aside.

"You should wear heels," Reina said, looking her over critically after she'd changed.

"I hate wearing heels," Julienne said.

Reina pouted.

"Just because you don't get to dress up," Julienne said, rolling her eyes.

Reina held up a pair of low black heels she'd found somewhere. "Try them on?"

Julienne put them on and then looked at herself in the mirror. She looked a little less tired in pants and a blouse, and the heels made her a little taller than Reina.

"You look great," Reina said.

Julienne sighed. "I feel like I need a lawyer for this meeting."

"C'mon," Reina said. "You got this."

Julienne nodded. She stood up a little straighter.

Then she remembered she had to go down three flights of stairs in heels to get to her car, and she slumped again.

"Hey," Reina said, checking her phone. "I have to go. My manager moved my flight up. But good luck, and tell me how it goes."

"You're leaving already?"

Reina nodded, biting her lip. "Some sports magazine wants an interview before the next tournament. It's nothing major, but it means someone is taking notice."

"That's great news, Ray."

"Thanks," Reina said. She gave Julienne a quick, tight hug.

Julienne didn't say much as they left the apartment. She was a little thrown off balance by Reina announcing her sudden disappearance. She'd expected Reina to be there when she came out, that she'd be able to debrief from whatever this meeting turned out to be.

They hugged once more, and Reina promised to keep in touch better, and then her car rumbled away from the curb, leaving Julienne staring after it.

There was no more putting it off. She had to deal with whatever Reina had got her into.

FOUR

She pressed the buzzer labelled Harper & Perez Management and gave her name and waited for the glass door to swing open to let her in. She rode the lift to the third floor and introduced herself to the receptionist, who directed her to the leather sofa in the waiting room. Nondescript art in muted tones decorated the wall; the room felt expensive and carefully designed.

"Julienne," Sadie said, only moments after Julienne had sat down. "I'm so glad you came. Would you like a drink?"

"Water, thank you," Julienne said, standing and reaching to shake Sadie's hand.

She followed Sadie to her office. Sadie poured her a glass of water from the jug on her desk.

"We'll start with the paperwork," Sadie said, once she was sat at her desk. "The non-disclosure agreement covers everything we discuss about your role and about the client. Take a minute to read and sign them, and let me know if you have any questions. Did you bring your résumé? I'd like to see it now."

Julienne pulled her résumé out of the folder she'd

brought it in. She hadn't had time to tweak it, she'd just grabbed the most recent copy she had. She handed it to Sadie, and Sadie pushed the paperwork across the desk and held out a pen.

Julienne began to read. It wasn't a long document, and although she'd never seen an NDA before, there wasn't anything in the wording that alarmed her. It didn't seem like Sadie, or Harper & Perez Management, were trying to deceive her. She scrawled a signature and pushed the document back to Sadie, sitting back in her chair.

Her palms were damp with sweat.

Sadie glanced at the document before filing it into a drawer, her résumé going alongside it. "My client's name is Cece Browne. You're aware she attends your gym?"

Julienne blinked and gave a jerky nod. For all their joking about it, she hadn't expected it to actually be Cece Browne.

"I'm her manager and in charge of her public relations. She also has an agent who represents her."

"What's my role in all this?" Julienne asked.

Sadie smiled at her, but it was a little joyless. She looked tired. "Cece has a promising career. Last award season, Bare Windows was nominated in 4 categories. She's got a movie coming out, she's talented, we want to make sure she has the best possible chance of success."

"Okay," Julienne said slowly. She'd heard of Bare Windows. It was one of those hyped shows everyone was talking about, prestige TV. She hadn't got around to watching it, but she knew Tori was a fan.

"She's struggling," Sadie said. "The biggest headline after the Emmys was an alleged fight between Cece and another actress at an after party."

Julienne didn't know what to say to that. She had a

feeling the word 'alleged' was doing a lot of work in that sentence.

"She needs a friend. Someone not interested in fame, who can keep an eye on her, keep her from spinning out of control. Stop people taking photos of her, stop her from sabotaging her own career."

"You want to hire me to be her friend?" Julienne asked. She wasn't sure why Sadie had asked for her résumé. It didn't seem like this was the kind of job anyone but a therapist was qualified for, and Julienne's collection of business internships and part-time jobs definitely didn't put her in a strong position.

"It's a little more complicated than that, but yes. She needs someone her own age who can look out for her interests. She doesn't want me breathing down her neck every day, and you can accompany her to parties without it seeming suspicious."

"Why don't you just ban her from going to parties?" Julienne asked.

Sadie gave her a look. "She's a nineteen year old who hasn't had a parental figure in her life for years. She won't listen to me."

"So what am I supposed to do?

"Stop things getting out of hand," Sadie said calmly.

Julienne looked blankly at her. That seemed like a lot of responsibility to take on, and who knew how willing Cece would be to listen? Just from seeing her at the gym, Julienne could tell she was strong-willed.

"You would be well compensated for your time," Sadie said. "It's not a standard 9 to 5 job, and we understand that."

Julienne swallowed. "How long is the contract?"

It was strange. She'd rehearsed this kind of conversation

in her head, for when she did finally have that successful interview and get a job offer, any job offer. She hadn't expected it to come out of left field like this; this conversation wasn't going according to any kind of plan.

Sadie considered her. "I don't want someone who will drop out of Cece's life at the first sign of trouble."

"I get that," Julienne said, inwardly wincing at her phrasing. She wanted to sound like a polished professional, but this conversation made that so difficult. "But this isn't exactly what I planned for my career."

"Think of it as a personal assistant role that's more focused on emotional support," Sadie said. "If you're interested in going into PR or management I can get you meetings and interviews when you're ready to move on. And we can call the first month a trial month, if you want. You'll get a bonus upon completion, but no penalties if you walk away."

Julienne nodded. Sadie probably did have the kind of connections Julienne would need to get a foot in the door in LA. She might finally get someone to take a chance on her, with Sadie's help.

"How does Cece feel about this?" Julienne asked. "She's happy for you to hire a babysitter for her?"

"It's the culmination of a long series of discussions that I'm sure she would prefer I not discuss with you," Sadie said. "It was a solution we reached together."

Julienne took a deep breath. She was running out of excuses to say no. She needed a job, and if it didn't work out, she could leave. Taking this job, staying in LA, was the sensible choice. Julienne had always prided herself on making the sensible choice.

She thought of her parents' email, the offer they'd made

to pay for her plane ticket home. She thought of the town, the life she'd be going back to.

"Why me?" she asked.

Sadie smiled, like she'd been waiting for that question. "Cece had a few stipulations. She didn't want it to be a therapist or anyone who'd treat her like a patient."

Julienne nodded. "Like a person, not a problem to be solved."

"Exactly," Sadie said. "She wanted it to be someone around her age, so there weren't any difficult questions to answer."

Sadie paused, and Julienne waited, sensing there was more to come.

"She actually suggested you," Sadie said.

Julienne's heart skipped a beat. Sadie looked pleased, like she'd been waiting to say that for the whole meeting. It was her winning play, and she knew it.

Nobody had ever noticed Julienne before. Least of all a celebrity.

She didn't know what to do with that information.

Sadie opened a drawer and pulled out another set of paperwork, pushing it over to Julienne.

"This is a one time offer," she said.

Now or never. Julienne swallowed. She looked down at the papers in front of her, trying to make a decision. Maybe she could help Cece. If she walked away from this, she would never know.

She skimmed the paperwork, and spotted the number she'd be paid. Her eyes watered. It was a lot of money, more than most of the jobs she was getting rejected from. Even if it didn't work out, a few months of this job would give her savings to keep living in LA and looking for work.

And the connections that Harper & Perez offered were vast.

It was the opportunity she'd been waiting for. That's what she told herself.

She swallowed and scrawled a signature on the dotted line. She couldn't make eye contact with Sadie. She felt a little ashamed by how easily she'd been convinced.

"Why don't we start on familiar territory?" Sadie said, smiling a little as she spoke. "I'll book a training room at the gym on Monday and you can start getting to know her there. If you give the receptionist your email I'll have them get in touch with the rest of the paperwork."

Julienne nodded. She was running on autopilot as she took a copy of the contract and NDA Sadie handed her. She was sure there were other questions she was supposed to ask, but her mind felt oddly blank. She gave her details to the receptionist and drove home.

She had a job. A job that paid real money.

All she had to do was figure out Cece Browne.

FIVE

The weekend swam by in a daze. Julienne did all her laundry, feeling unprepared for starting a brand new job, and called Reina to let her know she'd taken the job but couldn't tell her anything about it. Tori got the same spiel, and was way more sceptical about it than Reina was, but was too busy with her own work to press the issue.

By the time Monday came, Julienne felt a little like she'd spent the weekend with cotton wool in her ears, isolating from the world. There was a pit of dread in her stomach as she dressed. She didn't quite dress for a job interview, but she dressed up from what she would normally wear to the gym. She needed this to go well.

The sun shone on the shiny glass walls of the gym, making it hard to see into the reception. She didn't know if Sadie or Cece or both would be waiting for her, or if the receptionist would just send her to the meeting room to wait alone.

She smiled at the receptionist as she entered and decided, based on her early arrival, to wait in the lounge chairs nearby. She'd brought her gym bag, in case they were going to work out together or something, and apart from this meeting she had no idea what she was expected to do with Cece. She wanted to be prepared for everything, but she had no information.

She was more than a little nervous.

She fiddled with her phone. Not being able to text anyone what was happening was harder than she thought it would be. Mia would have been delighted to get a text about a meeting with Cece Browne. Julienne wondered if she would get to go to the set of Bare Windows at all – that would take Mia from delighted to green with jealousy.

Scrolling through social media did nothing to improve her mood. She was flicking from one app to the next when the door opened and Cece Browne bounced in. Julienne took in her appearance, trying to match up what she'd been told about Cece with the person in front of her.

Cece was one of those small people that looked tall, all quick limbs and confidence. Her hair was tight golden blonde curls, bouncing around her head like a halo. She grinned at the receptionist, said something that made her laugh, and then spotted Julienne sitting quietly in the corner.

Her smile turned a little wry and she eyed Julienne with open curiosity. Julienne felt pinned to the seat by it. She tried to forget that the last time she'd spoken to Cece she'd been wearing only a towel. The moment lasted achingly long before Cece was seemingly satisfied and headed over to her.

"Hey Julienne," she said brightly. "I'm gonna call you Jules."

Internally, Julienne groaned. She'd never been a fan of nicknames. "Nice to meet you again, Cece," she said.

"Is it?" Cece said.

Julienne blinked at her.

Cece gave her a quick, sharp grin, and the tension broke. She waved the key she was holding in her hand at Julienne. "Deanne gave me the keys to the training room," she said.

"Who's Deanne?" Julienne asked in spite of herself.

"The receptionist," Cece said, giving the woman in question a wave. She opened the door to the corridor and gestured Julienne through. "You come here like, every day, and you didn't know that?"

"I keep to myself," Julienne said. Being unemployed had made small talk painful, something Julienne had avoided at all costs the last few months.

"Sure," Cece said, walking briskly down one corridor and into another, leading Julienne to one of the personal training rooms. "This is us, anyways."

The room was set up for a trainer, with a scale and a foam roller in one corner and a set of free weights against the wall. It was oddly cool, and Julienne felt a shiver run down her spine as she entered. There was only one chair in the room and she shifted her weight from one foot to another, unsure of what she was supposed to be doing.

She swallowed nervously.

"Is Sadie coming?" she asked.

Cece shrugged. "She's usually pretty hands off, she'll probably leave us to it."

"This arrangement isn't really what I'd call hands off," Julienne said.

"Good point," Cece said. She dropped herself into the chair, and Julienne was starting to get the impression that everything Cece did, she did with a flourish.

Julienne was usually a little more confident meeting new people, but some combination of the situation and the way Cece's personality seemed to fill the whole room had her caving in on herself a little bit. It was so easy to see why she was famous, why she had fans. Her presence in a room was compelling.

"I'd love to know more about you," Cece said. "We're going to be spending a lot of time together."

Julienne tried to remember to breathe, like this was a normal job. Cece Browne wasn't a wayward celebrity, this meeting wasn't strictly protected by an NDA. "I'm twenty-two and I just graduated from UCLA. I majored in business and minored in art history, and I want to work in the arts someday." It was her standard patter, the basic introduction she gave at a job interview before talking about her work experience.

Cece nodded, but Julienne couldn't help but think that she looked a little bored. "What about like, the rest of you?" She gestured vaguely at the air.

Julienne drew a blank for a second, then: "I played tennis in college. I watch a lot of documentaries." She couldn't help but wonder if she was too boring for Cece.

Cece made a contemplative noise, a sort of hum that rang out into the room. "So why did you take the job?"

Julienne took a deep breath. "Um," she said. She shook her head, trying to get into her job interview headspace. "I hadn't really considered this kind of work before Sadie offered it to me," she began, and Cece's face drifted into a scowl. Julienne didn't understand how an actress could display every emotion she was feeling so clearly.

"Don't give me that shit," Cece said, a smile playing on her lips. "I want a real answer. I want to get to know the real you."

"I love LA and I need a job to stay," Julienne blurted out. "I want to see where it goes."

"So you've got nothing better going on, then," Cece said, but it sounded more teasing than begrudging. It didn't stop the flush of shame Julienne felt on the nape of her neck.

"It's not like anything else I've applied for," she said.

Cece shrugged. "We couldn't really advertise this in public. Young star destroying her own career, send help."

"Destroying your career?"

Cece furrowed her brow. "Sadie's words, not mine. She's always planning for the worst case scenario."

"She didn't give me any details," Julienne said, choosing her words carefully. "You had some bad press and needed some support."

"We both know you read between the lines of that," Cece said.

Julienne found herself wanting to please Cece, wanting to impress her. She struggled with her words for a moment. "I don't want to assume anything," she said. "What do you think you need?"

"Someone to stop anyone taking a photo of me when I'm drunk," Cece said, her voice going a little rough. Already, Julienne missed the smile on her face.

Julienne bit her lip. That seemed like a much more focused job description than the one Sadie had given her – and one she wasn't sure she was comfortable filling. "Am I wasting my time? If you just want a bodyguard I'm not that person."

Cece shrugged. She looked petulant, and even though she was only three years younger than Julienne, the gap seemed vast. Julienne tried to remember who she'd been at nineteen, but she wasn't sure there was any use comparing her life with someone like Cece's.

"Sadie said you needed a friend," Julienne said, keeping

her voice soft as she tried a different tack. She didn't want to blow it on the first day.

There was a beat of silence, and Julienne couldn't read the expression on Cece's face. "I guess that's true enough," she said. "A friend who won't encourage my bad decisions. Someone who doesn't want to be famous or sell stories about me."

"That's me, I guess."

Cece nodded. She seemed to be considering Julienne. "Tell you what," she said. "Let's start by just hanging out for a few days, like we're actually friends. See where that gets us."

Julienne gave an uncertain nod. It was close enough to what Sadie had asked her to do and it would be a good chance to actually get to know Cece. She wasn't sure if she should be reassured by the fact that Cece seemingly had no idea how to do this, either. It made her like Cece, instantly, that she was just finding her way through this the same as Julienne; that they were coming from two different angles and meeting in the middle. And Cece was treating her better than any job interviewer ever had: she felt like a person, not a résumé being assessed.

"What are you going to tell people about who I am?" Julienne asked.

Cece thought about it for a second. "If you were my personal trainer I'd have an excuse to fire Jacob, but it would be weird if you came to parties."

Cece seemed to be thinking aloud, not really needing Julienne's input. "We can just say we're friends, for now."

"It's closest to the truth," Julienne said. "You could even say Sadie introduced us."

Cece nodded, already moving on to something else and sliding her phone out of her pocket, checking the time. She stood up, bouncing a little on her heels. "I'll show you around set this afternoon if you want," she said. She paused. "There's a party tonight, too."

She looked Julienne up and down, considering her. Julienne suddenly felt self-conscious.

"We'll have to get you out of those clothes," Cece said. She smirked. "C'mon, we'll go to set and then drop by my place. Did you drive here?"

"No," Julienne said. She was a little thrown off by that smirk. Something that might have been one, lonely butterfly stirred in her stomach. She told herself it was just that being the focus of Cece's attention was overwhelming, that Cece's smirk seemed so confident and knowing. That was all it was, nothing more.

"Perfect," Cece said. She spun her keys, which had materialised from somewhere, around her fingers. "Let's go."

Julienne followed, feeling half-a-step behind and slightly off kilter. She had a feeling Cece had that effect on people.

SIX

The set was in an area of town Julienne hadn't been to before, and it was busy with people as soon as they arrived. People seemed to steer clear of the two of them – Julienne even saw someone spot Cece and turn on their heel. She had to wonder what had happened to cause that kind of reaction.

"We can hang out in my trailer for a bit," Cece said, leading her to a lot behind the building.

"What are you filming today?" Julienne asked, looking around.

Cece frowned. "I think it's episode six? Bare Windows, season two."

Cece gave the door of the trailer a tug and it swung open. The carpet inside looked lush, the lighting soft. There were some pictures stuck on the inside of the windows, but Julienne didn't look at them too closely as Cece ushered her inside the trailer, directing her to sit on the soft leather sofa. It was more luxury than Julienne had seen in a while.

"This is nice," Julienne said.

Cece rolled her eyes. "Nice is such a platitude. You're way too polite, y'know."

Julienne blinked. "What do you want me to say?" she asked.

Cece shrugged, using her whole body to make the gesture. "I don't know," she said. "If we're going to be friends, you need to be real with me."

"This is me being real," Julienne said quietly. "I really do think it's nice in here."

Cece wrinkled her nose. "I suggested you because you seem like a normal person. You don't have to be nice to me all the time, that's not what this is." She bent down to take a bottle of water from the mini fridge. She tossed one to Julienne, who barely managed to catch it, and then took a long swig from her own.

Everything about her was commanding. Earlier, Cece's personality had filled the meeting room they were in; in her trailer, Julienne felt dwarfed by it.

"This is a weird situation," Julienne said. "Give me a minute to get used to it."

Why was she so intimidated by a girl smaller than her, younger than her, wilder than her? She'd been around extroverts before, people more successful than her – her best friend was Reina, of course she had. She should be able to handle Cece fine, but here she was, wide-eyed and nervous.

"Yeah," Cece said, conceding. "Here's hoping you loosen up at the party tonight."

Julienne didn't know what to say to that, either. "Whose party is it?"

Cece shrugged. She'd emptied her water already and crumpled the bottle in her fist, tossing it in a recycling bin in the corner. "Someone famous-ish," she said. "I'll introduce you 'round."

Julienne shifted uncomfortably on the couch. She didn't know if she was ready to be introduced around by Cece. She had to figure out how to fit-in at a party full of people who were 'famous-ish'. Already she was starting to worry that this job was more than she'd bargained for. She was ordinary, just a college graduate trying to find her place. She didn't go to wild parties with celebrities. That wasn't who she was.

"C'mon, I need to talk to Sam," Cece said. She grabbed a stack of papers from her desk and looked around the trailer. "Wait, if you want anything for lunch you should check the fridge, we probably won't stop to eat."

"You're not going to eat?" Julienne asked. She opened the fridge and pulled a face at the contents. A few pre-made salads, well past their use-by dates, a single yogurt, and a lot of water. "Who's Sam?"

"Not hungry," Cece said. Julienne closed the door of the fridge. "Sam's the showrunner, everyone's boss. He wants to fire me," she said, opening the trailer door and stepping out without looking back.

Julienne blinked. She hurried after her, wishing Cece would slow down so she could actually form a response to the things she said. She wondered if she should be taking notes. She had a feeling there was a lot to know about Cece and she was not prepared for this crash course.

Cece was already ten paces ahead of her, her shoulders set in a stern line. She'd blown through two doors by the time Julienne caught up with her, and someone with a clipboard had appeared at her elbow.

"Not now," Cece said, her tone sharper than Julienne had heard it.

Julienne didn't know what to say to Cece. She hadn't

even realised there was a storm brewing, but now Cece was clearly furious.

The clipboard girl stayed with her as she crossed the set, just barely dodging around the cameras. They were clearly gearing up to film, and Julienne tried not to notice the Oscar-winning actress waiting for her scene.

The rest of the crew looked irritated by Cece marching through the set. She didn't bother knocking before bursting into an office, dropping her bag of papers on the desk with a thump.

"He's busy," an assistant said, leaping up from his desk. "You can't storm in here."

Cece crossed her arms across her chest. "I'm not leaving till he talks to me," she said.

The assistant heaved a heavy sigh and picked up his phone. There was a brief conversation, and then he gestured Cece through the door behind him.

Julienne followed and closed the door behind her.

"You are trying to write me out of the show," Cece said, her voice quiet but furious.

"Have you been drinking?" the man asked, his voice gravelly. He didn't look surprised to see Cece.

"It's like 12, I'm not an alcoholic," Cece said.

He shrugged. "Who's your friend?" he asked.

"Oh," Cece said. "Sam, this is Julienne, hired by Sadie to keep an eye on me. Julienne, this is Sam, the bane of my existence."

"Also known as the executive producer of this show," Sam said, rolling his eyes. "I am your boss, and you keep screwing up. There are consequences for that."

"So you're just going to get rid of me?" Cece said. "That's what this script feels like."

"It's an option we are keeping on the table," Sam said.

"You are not the star of the show, Cece, and there are a whole lot of people here who need to do their jobs. Every time you slow production down, it costs us money and time. Be thankful we didn't just kill Anna."

Cece scowled. Julienne wanted to shrink into the shadow of the doorway. She assumed Anna was Cece's character, and that was why she was so furious.

"Sit down," Sam said. He glanced at Julienne. "Both of you."

Julienne swallowed and took a seat next to Cece.

"You're a good kid, Cece, but you've got to get your shit together. Showing up too hungover to work, or high or coming down, whatever it is. It needs to stop. You're not irreplaceable."

Cece didn't say anything. Julienne didn't dare look at her face.

"Honestly?" Sam said. "We can handle some bad publicity. The Emmys thing? Don't sweat it. But delaying production isn't okay. There are people far more important and expensive than you are who have to work longer hours because of it."

"I don't do it on purpose," Cece said, her voice small.

Sam raised his eyebrows. "You don't try hard not to."

"Julienne's going to help," Cece said. "I'm going to try."

They both looked at Julienne and waited.

Her mind went blank. She barely knew what her job was supposed to be, and now she had to convince the executive producer of an award-winning show.

She swallowed. "I'm going to do what I can to keep her out of trouble," she said.

"Are you going to get her into work on time? Stop her from arguing? Make sure she's not coming down from something?"

Julienne took a deep breath. "I don't want to make promises I can't keep," she said. "But I'll try."

"Alright," Sam said. He considered the papers Cece had left on his desk. "I'm not changing the script back. You get your act in gear, we'll revisit the plan for season three."

Cece nodded. She opened her mouth, then closed it again with a click.

Julienne wondered if she was trying not to argue.

"You know your schedule for the next few days?" he asked

Cece nodded again.

"Alright. Don't storm into my office again."

"I make no promises," Cece said, her cheeky grin returning.

Sam sighed. "I'm just trying to do my job, Cece." He made a dismissive hand gesture and Cece stood up. Julienne followed.

"It's a pretty short scene I have to film this afternoon," Cece said, walking at a brisk pace through set, not looking at anyone. "Then we can go to mine, get you all dressed up, and go to the party."

"You're still going to the party after that?" Julienne asked.

"I need something to cheer me up," Cece said. "Don't you?"

"Do you have work tomorrow?" Julienne asked.

Cece led her to the makeup trailer, dropping herself in a chair, and Julienne stood back to allow the makeup artist to work. "Yeah," she said, closing her eyes.

"Don't you want to show him you're making an effort?" Julienne asked. She didn't want to push too hard, not on the first day, but... Sam had made it clear what the stakes were.

"Sure," Cece said. "So I won't get wasted. I still need to show you around."

Julienne closed her mouth. The silence hung in the air for a second.

She didn't know how she was supposed to intervene.

She was completely at a loss.

SEVEN

"You can wait in the trailer or you can watch," Cece said, walking towards the set. It was set out like an all-American living room, and it reminded Julienne a little of where she'd spent her early childhood. She trailed behind Cece as she grabbed a script from somewhere and approached someone to discuss it.

Julienne didn't know where to look. She'd never been in the same room as anyone famous.

She wished she could text someone about it, but the terms of the non-disclosure agreement were pretty clear.

She stood a little awkwardly a few paces behind Cece, watching as the crew got set up and the director gave instructions. There was a hive of activity around the set, and it was the first time she'd ever got a behind the scenes look at any kind of production. Her dad was a film buff and would have been so jealous of her getting to see this, spend actual time behind the scenes. She could picture him pointing people out to her, explaining what the camera crew were doing, just absolutely in his element.

It was a shame she couldn't tell him anything about it.

She hadn't thought of that aspect of the non-disclosure agreement when she'd signed it.

Several things seemed to happen at once, and the hive of activity around the room became very focused and still. Cece appeared in front of the lights, script still in hand, but she looked different. Julienne didn't know when she'd had time to get changed, but it wasn't just that. She was carrying herself differently, the expression on her face entirely different that the versions of Cece Julienne had already met.

A woman with a clipboard took the script from her and Cece moved to the back of the set, through a closed door. Ellary Markson, an actress who Julienne mostly knew through gifs of her at award shows, took her place on set, along with a man Julienne didn't recognise.

The director called out: "Action!"

From her spot in the corner, out of the way, Julienne couldn't quite hear what was going on. Cece looked every bit the petulant teenager as some conversation happened. It surprised Julienne, how quickly the scene in front of her became real; as if she was just watching Cece interact with her mother from a distance.

The scene finished and the director stepped in to have a brief conversation. They set up for another take, and Julienne moved a little closer, trying to hear what was going on.

She tried to measure the differences between the Cece on set and the Cece she'd spent the morning with. Even with the distraction of the camera crew, Julienne found herself totally wrapped up in the scene. There was something magic about the way Cece transformed. Even when the focus was on her parents, Cece's body language told its own story in the background, frustrated with the situation her character had found herself in.

They filmed variations on the same scene for two hours, occasionally taking breaks to touch up hair and makeup. Julienne only managed to figure out some of the characters' names in that time; she still didn't really have a handle on what the show was about.

They stopped to take a break, and the crew dispersed around the room. It took Julienne a second to realise Cece had disappeared from view.

She headed for Cece's trailer, knocking cautiously on the door.

"Just a sec," Cece's voice called out. A few moments passed and then Cece opened the door.

"Oh, it's you," she said.

"Sorry to disappoint," Julienne said.

Cece blinked at her, amusement written on her face for just a moment before it disappeared. She'd gotten changed into her clothes from earlier, a pair of jeans and a faded blue t-shirt. She looked more relaxed than Julienne had seen her all day. "Ready to go?"

Julienne nodded, as if her whole day so far hadn't been following Cece around. As if she had any other reason to be on the set of Bare Windows.

It wasn't a long drive to Cece's place in West Hollywood, and Cece for once didn't seem bothered with conversation. She pulled into a covered driveway and got out.

The condo was set back from the road, the walk up to it paved over with terracotta tiles. There were some plants by the entrance, though they looked a little worse for wear. Julienne wondered if she could find out what kind they were and bring them back to life. She'd managed to revive a pot plant a dormmate had been gifted in Junior year, and it still lived on her desk in her apartment.

"This is me," Cece said, opening the door. It wouldn't

open all the way, and once Julienne was inside she realised there was a pile of unopened mail blocking it, some of it marked with footprints.

She thought about pointing it out, but Cece just carried straight on upstairs. Julienne didn't get a chance to pause and look around, but what she glimpsed of the ground floor was open-plan and modern, light wooden floors and pale walls. It would have been minimalist if it wasn't littered with papers and clutter.

She followed Cece upstairs, finding a bare corridor with a few white doors off it.

"I guess you can sleep in there," Cece said, gesturing to one of the closed doors, before walking through the open doorway into her own room.

Julienne blinked at her. "Why would I sleep here?"

Cece shrugged. "You promised Sam you'd get me to work on time, didn't you?"

Cece's room was dominated by an unmade bed, the sheets creamy white. One whole wall was a window, blinds pulled down, and the other was mostly made up of a mirror.

Julienne felt like she was losing control of her life. This job seemed to be tugging at the edges of her routine and taking it apart.

"Just for tonight," she said.

Cece met her eyes and smirked. "Sure."

The room was oddly impersonal. Cece's trailer on set had seemed to have more personality than her bedroom. Julienne wondered why there weren't any pictures on the walls. There was no indication that the person who lived here had friends or a life, and that worried Julienne a little. It wasn't what she'd expected from Cece.

"The party isn't for a few hours," Cece said. "Do you want to order some food? I'll pay."

Cece ran her hand over the sheets for a moment until she found an iPad and tossed it to Julienne. "I've got all the apps installed, pick whatever."

"You don't want anything?"

Cece shrugged. "Tell me where you end up ordering from and I might add something, it depends."

Julienne tried to remember if she'd seen Cece eat anything at all today. She didn't know if she should be worried about an eating disorder, or if Cece just didn't really care about looking after herself. She thought about asking, but Cece was already distracted, browsing the walk-in wardrobe attached to her bedroom. Julienne tapped through the menus till she found something she liked and then passed it back to Cece. Cece added something to the order and then handed it back.

"Put your number in it," she said. "How short of a skirt are you cool with wearing?"

"What?" Julienne asked, not following the sharp turn in conversation.

Cece leaned out of the closet to meet her eyes. "You need to change for the party," she said, like it was not up for debate.

Julienne put the tablet down on the bedspread, her contact information saved.

"C'mon," Cece said. "We're probably the same size, you can pick whatever."

Julienne moved closer to the closet, taking in the packed rails of clothing. "Wow."

Cece shrugged. "I don't wear most of it."

"I mostly wear shorts," Julienne said. Skirts just reminded her of her tennis uniform, and shorts always made her feel a little more relaxed.

Cece turned and looked her up and down. Julienne

fought the urge to hunch her shoulders and make herself smaller. The full force of Cece's attention made her want to shrink.

"You'll have to pair it with something shiny," Cece said, decisively. "That section is everything glitter."

Julienne bit down on a laugh at that. She hadn't realised it was possible to have an entire rack dedicated to glitter, but there was a lot of silver and gold and multicoloured sparkle.

"What are you wearing?" Julienne asked.

She was a little nervous to check the labels on the shirts. She didn't own anything designer, and she wasn't sure she'd seen clothes this expensive in real life before. She and Tori were far more likely to hit up a thrift store than anywhere else.

She tugged out a button-up from the rail and considered it. It wasn't entirely made of glitter, like some of the clothes seemed to be, but it was a soft grey material and woven with threads of silver. She held it up to herself and turned around to Cece.

Her words caught in her throat before she could ask Cece's opinion. Cece was topless and shimmying out of her trousers. It was an effort for Julienne to make eye contact; her mouth was dry and her heartbeat thudded in her ears.

Cece stood up straight, unbothered. "That looks cute," she said. Julienne felt her cheeks grow warm. "I'm just wearing jeans, I think."

Julienne's brain stuttered, unable to keep from picturing Cece topless at a party. "Just jeans? Nothing else?"

"And a crop top," Cece said. Julienne noticed she had freckles across her shoulders. She tried not to stare. It took her a moment to notice that Cece was smirking at her.

"I'm going to check on our food," Julienne said. The

closet had felt huge a minute ago, but now it was too small and too warm.

She was sure she was flushed.

"Sure," Cece said, her voice entirely too casual.

Julienne picked up the iPad and checked their order status, trying not to think about the taut lines of Cece's body. Being attracted to Cece Browne was not part of her job description. It definitely wasn't going to make this job any easier.

Cece re-emerged from the closet wearing a black t-shirt, and Julienne hoped her sigh of relief wasn't visible.

"Tell me about the party tonight," Julienne said, sitting cross-legged on the bed.

Cece brightened. "So it's this former Nickelodeon girl who always throws ridiculous parties. Her house is like, designed for it. There's a DJ booth in the backyard."

"So it'll be a lot of celebrities?"

Cece tilted her head to one side, considering the question. "I mean, no one huge. We're talking like, Teen Choice Award crowd. People who can still play teenagers on TV."

"I don't watch the Teen Choice Awards," Julienne said.

Cece smirked. Julienne was starting to realise that was her trademark. "Barely anybody does. Don't worry, I'll introduce you to the important people."

"I'm mostly used to college parties," Julienne said. "This side of LA is totally new to me."

"It's just a lot of young hot people with too much money," Cece said. She shrugged. "There's a ton of money in being young and hot."

Julienne didn't know what to say to that. She'd expected Cece to be a young celebrity who was all caught up in being a star, drunk on all the attention, but Cece was surprisingly cynical.

"Speaking of," Cece said. "Can you take some photos? Sadie said I need to post more when I'm filming."

"Sure," Julienne said. Cece handed her phone, and Julienne took it a little gingerly. It didn't even have a passcode, and Julienne wasn't sure she was ready to be trusted with Cece's Instagram account.

Cece struck a pose, giving the camera a sultry smile. Julienne took a photo, and Cece moved quickly into a new pose, trying various ways to lounge against the white sheets.

Julienne tried not to let her eyes linger on the bare skin of Cece's legs as she snapped the photos.

Cece started to direct her more, telling Julienne where she should stand to get the right angles. Julienne probably took fifteen photos before Cece put an end to it and held out her hand for the phone. Julienne sat beside her and watched as she flicked through the photos and chose a few, adding filters as she went.

They were briefly interrupted by the arrival of the food they'd ordered, and Julienne left Cece to her editing as she answered the door. She found some cutlery by the sink in the kitchen and brought it upstairs with the rest of the food.

Cece was still fiddling with her phone on the bed, and Julienne hesitated, reluctant to put the containers on the white sheets and stain them. She put the bag on the nightstand and started unpacking it.

"You don't have a social media manager?" she asked, trying to decide if she should eat standing up or not.

Cece looked up from her phone. "Oh, food," she said. "Nah, Sadie lets me handle it, and if I fuck up she just changes my password and kicks me out for a couple days."

"What do you get kicked out for?"

"Tweeting when I'm drunk, getting into fights." She

paused, and looked at Julienne. "You can eat on the bed if you want, I don't mind. Bring mine over."

Julienne tried not to bristle at being treated as Cece's assistant. She passed Cece her container.

"You're going to make the sheets gross," she said. Something about the clean white sheets being spoiled by Thai food just felt wrong to Julienne.

"Okay, mom," Cece said, laughing. "My cleaner is coming tomorrow, it'll be fine."

Cece pressed a button on her phone and music came out of a hidden set of speakers as they ate. It filled the silence a little. Holding a conversation with Cece was harder than Julienne thought it would be. She hoped it was just that they were still getting to know each other, feeling out each other's boundaries. She hoped it would get easier.

"We should get ready to leave soon," Cece said, finishing her noodles and sliding off the bed. "We can take a selfie together at the party if you want, get you some more followers."

"Doesn't that miss the point of the NDA?" Julienne asked. She wasn't looking for more followers; it wasn't something she expected Cece to give her.

Cece shrugged. She pulled off her shirt as she walked into the dressing room, and Julienne tried to fight the heat she could feel rising to her face.

She emerged moments later in a crop top so small it barely covered her chest and jeans that clung to her hips.

Julienne couldn't help but watch as Cece examined herself in the mirror, hands on her hips. She pushed at the curls of her hair and sank to the floor to rummage in her makeup bag.

"You're not getting ready," she said, mascara wand in hand.

Julienne blinked. Her mouth was dry, her cheeks were hot.

"Sorry," she said, snapping out of it. She felt shame trickle down her spine, and she turned away from Cece to undress. She wished she'd been warned about how bold Cece was, happy to prance around in her underwear. She hadn't realised how close they would be. She shook herself, trying not to think about the shape of Cece's breasts in her bra.

Cece's silver blouse fit Julienne perfectly, and the shorts were a little loose on her narrow hips. She tucked the shirt in to fill the space, and left the top few buttons undone.

"That's cute," Cece said. Julienne turned quickly, uncomfortable with being watched.

"Thanks," Julienne said. She shifted from one foot to another, a little uneasy.

"I'm ready, I think. Shall I order an Uber?"

Julienne looked in the mirror and ran a hand through her hair. Standing side by side with Cece, it felt obvious which of them was the celebrity. She felt like no one.

She might as well be invisible.

EIGHT

It wasn't long before Cece was bounding out the door, back to her highest energy level. Julienne tried not to feel weird about leaving stacks of plates on the bedside table, and as she walked out she realised she hadn't even looked at the room she was supposed to be sleeping in.

She tried to tamp down on her anxieties during the drive over. It wasn't a long drive, but Cece still found time to flip through the radio stations until she found an appropriate song.

"We didn't pre-game," Cece said, turning around to talk to Julienne in the back seat. "We'll probably be the most sober people there."

"I'm not going to drink," Julienne said. It was the sensible thing to do, she told herself.

Cece only paused for a beat to blink at her before she carried on. "Oh, and we should sync our calendars. You'll need to know what my schedule looks like."

Cece leapt out of the car as soon as they arrived. From the outside, it looked similar to Cece's place but bigger, like everything was scaled up. Julienne wondered what it was like to be young and able to afford a house like this in LA. Her apartment in downtown Hollywood seemed a thousand miles away.

Already, Cece was paces ahead of her, and Julienne wondered if she'd ever not be running to catch up.

As she got close to the house, she began to feel the thrum of the bass vibrating through her. Light spilled out of the open front door, and by the time she was inside the brightly lit foyer, Cece was already having a conversation.

"This is my friend, Jules," Cece said.

"It's Julienne," she said, but she got the sense that nobody really cared.

Nobody else introduced themselves, and the conversation carried on as if it hadn't been interrupted.

Cece passed her a water bottle and she took a swig. Cece was drinking something from a blue solo cup.

"I'm gonna go talk to some people," Cece said to the group, and Julienne only had time to blink before Cece wrapped her fingers around Julienne's wrist and tugged her away. They ventured further into the house, pausing by a table full of bottles of expensive-looking alcohol so Cece could make herself a second drink.

"You sure you don't want to drink?" Cece asked.

"I'm working," Julienne said.

Cece wrinkled her nose. "C'mon, let's go outside," she said. She pulled Julienne along, through another crowded room and out the back. The music was louder out here, but instead of heading for the throngs of people by the DJ booth Cece directed Julienne around the side of the house, towards some benches.

Julienne sat in a wooden seat and Cece perched on the arm, and she worried for a moment that they might look like a couple. She brushed the thought aside, trying to focus on doing her job.

Whatever that job was.

It was hard to ignore Cece taking up all the space right next to her, her body heat somehow making Julienne's hairs stand on end.

"Golden hour," Cece said, holding up her phone. "I promised you a photo."

"You didn't," Julienne said, but it didn't matter. Cece already had the camera app open.

Julienne put her water on the floor and out of sight. "What do you want me to do?" she asked. She assumed it would be a similar exercise to the earlier photoshoot.

"I'm just going to keep it simple," Cece said, "Just lounge in the chair and smile. You look hot."

Julienne blinked, her brain caught on Cece's last sentence.

"Lounge," Cece said firmly, and Julienne followed directions, leaning back in the chair and lifting her chin to look at the camera. "Perfect," Cece said, taking the photo.

Apparently, at parties, it only took one photo for Cece to be satisfied, and she quickly tapped through and posted it. "What's your handle?"

Julienne bit her lip. "Are you sure Sadie is okay with this?"

Cece rolled her eyes. "If you don't want me to post it, that's fine."

Julienne didn't want to get on Cece's bad side this early in the night. That seemed like a good way to start supervised partying on the wrong foot. She held out her hand for Cece's phone and Cece grinned, her eyes seeming to sparkle.

Julienne swallowed. She could get lost in those eyes if she wasn't careful. She typed in her account name on Cece's phone and then muted notifications on her own. She didn't really want to know what anyone had to say about the photo.

Cece hummed above her, still fiddling on her phone. "Your Instagram actually makes you look kind of fun," she said. "You were partying like, last week."

"A friend from college was in town," Julienne said.

"I knew you weren't boring," Cece said. "I could just tell." She grinned at her and then tugged a vape pen out of her pocket.

Julienne didn't know what to say to that. She just sat back and watched as Cece took a long inhale from the pen.

The tranquility was broken by a deep voice. "Cee!" A tall, lean boy with dark skin and a wide smile dropped himself in the chair opposite.

"Hey Josh," Cece said. She moved from the arm of Julienne's chair straight to the boy's lap and held out her vape to him. Her denim-clad legs dangled over the edge of the chair and the pose was more elegant than it had any right to be.

"Who's your friend?" he asked, before holding the pen to his lips and taking a long, slow drag.

"Joshua, this is Julienne. Julienne, this is my friend Joshua."

"Hi," Julienne said, as Joshua exhaled a plume of vapour.

Joshua nodded at her, still smiling, and passed the pen back to Cece. "How do you two know each other?"

Julienne looked at Cece first, who gave her a small shake of the head. "Sadie asked me to show her around town," Cece said.

Joshua laughed, loud and booming. "Sadie wouldn't trust you to show anyone around town."

Cece put on an exaggerated pout.

Joshua looked between them thoughtfully. "Am I interrupting a date? You know you can just tell me, Cee."

Julienne's mouth went dry and her mind blank, but Cece giggled. "I would never make one of my dates meet you," she said to Joshua.

He rolled his eyes and she blew him a kiss.

"How long have you guys been friends?" Julienne asked, though she was beginning to feel like she was the one third wheeling on their date.

"Since like, grade school," Cece said. "When my mom decided to try the homeschooling thing, we shared a tutor."

"Stage moms," Joshua said, rolling his eyes. "The things we do for fame."

"We've been pretty much joined at the hip ever since," Cece said.

Joshua nodded. "Thank god we've never worked together, though." He poked Cece in the ribs and she squirmed away from him, laughing. "I hear this one is a nightmare diva."

"I'm very easy to work with," Cece said. "I had a very reasonable discussion with Sam today."

Joshua raised his eyebrows.

"She stormed into his office," Julienne said.

He laughed. "You're going to get yourself fired one of these days," he told Cece.

Cece rolled her eyes and didn't say anything. Julienne wondered if that comment hit too close to home.

"So you're an actor too?" Julienne asked, trying to make conversation.

Joshua laughed. "I can't believe you don't recognise me," he said, with a flamboyant flick of his wrist.

"She probably doesn't watch gay porn, Joshy," Cece said.

"That's homophobic," Joshua said, his eyes twinkling with mirth. Julienne got the sense that this was a well-worn joke between them. "I don't do porn."

"He's a model," Cece told Julienne. "He nearly accidentally did porn once."

"I didn't read the ad properly," he said. "It was before I had proper representation. I used to act but I like modelling more."

"Standing still and looking pretty," Cece said, brushing a hand along Joshua's jawline.

Joshua grinned up at her. "What can I say, I'm a natural."

Cece smiled back. "Oh man," she said. "I just realised Julienne is probably the only person at this party who isn't trying to get famous."

"Everyone here wants to be famous?" Julienne said, looking around. Most people just seemed to be enjoying themselves, the music thumping a beat they could dance to.

"Pretty much," Joshua said. "Make connections, get pictures with them. It's part of the game."

"This is where the z-listers congregate," Cece said, exhaling another plume of sugary scented vapor.

"You guys seem pretty relaxed about it, though."

Joshua's smirk looked just like Cece's. "We're at the top of the trash heap, babe," he said.

Julienne raised an eyebrow.

Cece laughed. "He is, I just don't give a fuck."

Julienne took another sip of water. "So I guess I'm not the only person who isn't trying to get famous," she said.

"Oooh, she's got you there," Joshua said.

Cece pursed her lips. "Smarter than she looks," she said, and Joshua laughed.

Impulsively, Julienne stuck her tongue out at Cece, and Cece threw back her head and laughed.

"I like her," Joshua decided.

"She's okay, I guess," Cece said, still smiling. Julienne met her eyes. There it was again, that first flutter of butter-flies in her stomach.

She tried to ignore it. "I'm right here," she said. She couldn't look away from Cece.

There was a pause.

"Okay, now I feel like I'm interrupting a date," Joshua said, and the tension broke.

"You're too sensitive," Cece said, patting him on the chest. "I'm gonna get another drink, you want one?"

Joshua shook his head and Cece stood up and disappeared back into the house.

"We'll go looking for her if she's not back in ten," he said. "She's one of those people who always disappears at parties."

"You've really known her for that long?" Julienne asked.

He nodded. "So many years of drama," he said, faux-exhausted.

Julienne laughed. "I bet you have some great stories."

"Nuh uh," Joshua said. "Even though Cece vouched for you, I'm not giving you any dirt. Ask me again if you're still around in a month."

"You're no fun," she told him.

Joshua shrugged. "I've had excellent media training."

The conversation drifted to other things, and Julienne was in the middle of telling him about her favorite art gallery in LA when Cece returned, using a plastic frisbee as a drinks tray.

"A shot and a chaser," Cece said.

Julienne watched as they bumped their shot glasses against each other and threw them back.

"You're a bad influence," Joshua said.

Cece grinned. "Let's go dance." She held out her hand to him and pulled him up.

Julienne followed them into the crowd, the bass thumping beneath her feet. Cece cut a weaving path through the press of people, occasionally pausing to say hi to people she knew. In the dark, lasers shone into the crowd, and Julienne could almost get wrapped up in all of it and forget that she was sober and this party was unlike any she'd been to before.

There was a moment, when the three of them were dancing, when Cece's eyes met Julienne's and a shiver ran up her spine. There was heat in Cece's eyes, something Julienne hadn't expected to see, and she was suddenly very, very glad she was sober.

The moment didn't last. Julienne didn't know what changed, but Cece's face hardened and her jaw tensed. Julienne looked around for the cause, but a split second later, it didn't seem to matter anymore – Cece was already squaring up to someone.

Julienne tried to get to Cece, but the crowd moved between them and knocked into Julienne, and it took effort just to stay upright.

Joshua grabbed onto her wrist and pulled her close to him, and Julienne was grateful for the chance to breathe.

"You okay?" he said.

"I have to get to Cece," she said.

"She'll be fine," he said, but he still took hold of her

wrist and helped her make a path through the unforgiving crowd. Julienne didn't know when it had gotten so intense out there.

Cece and the girl were close to blows, Cece's mouth twisted in a snarl. It wasn't until Julienne saw her face up close that she realised how drunk Cece was.

"Leave me alone," Cece snarled. "You always try to start shit."

The girl wore a cruel smile on her face. She checked her nails, theatrically. "I'll just keep sweeping up your roles, then. We'll never have to see each other when your career is over."

"Shut the fuck up," Cece said, pushing forward. Julienne grabbed her arm to hold her back. She wasn't sure she was prepared to get in the middle of an actual fight. Preventing one from breaking out in the middle of a crowd was hard enough as it was.

Joshua had disappeared.

The woman appeared to notice Julienne holding onto her and a complicated expression crossed her face.

"Let me guess, someone else you're going to string along," she said to Cece.

"Cece," Julienne said, trying not to think about what the other woman meant. "She's looking for a fight."

"She's going to get one," Cece spat back.

"No, she's not," Julienne said, trying to keep her tone measured. "Who is she, even? She doesn't matter."

"I've been around a lot longer than *you* have," the woman said, speaking to Julienne this time. "And I plan to outlast Cece in this town, too."

"In your dreams," Cece said, her fists clenched and jaw tight with fury. Julienne tugged at her arm again. Cece didn't move, and Julienne shifted and stood in front of her, getting in between Cece and the other girl.

"Let's go," she said. "Forget it."

Cece looked past her, and for a second Julienne wasn't sure she'd even heard her. "Bitch," she said, over Julienne's shoulder, and then dipped her chin in a curt nod and let Julienne direct her out of the crowd and into the fresh air.

"You okay?" Julienne asked.

"Fine," Cece said tersely.

She didn't say anything else.

"Do you want some water?" Julienne asked.

"I'm not drunk," Cece said.

Julienne just looked at her.

"I'm not *that* drunk," Cece said.

"Who was that?" Julienne asked, changing tack.

Cece shrugged. "We have history. Every time I get a role or something, she pops up talking about how I don't deserve it. She's still bitter over some stuff that happened years ago and thinks she can ruin my career to get over it."

"Sounds... complicated," Julienne said. "What does Sadie think about it?"

Cece sighed with her whole body. "I don't know," she said. "We haven't really talked about it." She pulled her vape pen out of her pocket and took a long drag.

"I think we should call it a night," Julienne said softly.

Cece looked around, as if looking for a reason to stay. Detritus from the party was on the chairs they'd sat on earlier, and someone was singing off-key in the background. "Yeah, I guess," she said.

She looked smaller than Julienne had ever seen her.

She passed Julienne her phone to order a ride home and went all quiet, and Julienne didn't know what to do with that. She didn't know what to say to get her to open up.

Nothing about Cece was easy to figure out.

Cece curled in on herself when they got in the car and didn't speak for the whole ride home. It wasn't until she was unlocking her front door that she seemed to loosen up a little.

"Thanks," Cece said quietly. "I'm not used to someone looking out for me."

Julienne swallowed. She had to get this right, she knew, or the whole thing was pointless. "I'm only trying to help," she said.

Cece nodded. She looked exhausted, suddenly, and Julienne wanted to give her a hug.

"Your bed should be all made up," Cece said. "I've got to be at work at 12, so wake me up at 11, yeah?"

Julienne nodded. "Please drink some water," she said.

Cece rolled her eyes. "Sure."

"Sweet dreams," Julienne said.

Cece snorted.

"Goodnight, weirdo."

NINE

She started her second day at her new job tugging on yesterday's clothes and trying not to grimace when she saw her reflection in the mirror.

Even though she hadn't been drunk the previous night, she still felt groggy and tired. When she went downstairs she found the cupboards empty and the coffee machine broken.

She wanted to go home, have a smoothie, and go to the gym to work out her frustrations, but Cece had driven her over here and she wasn't sure if she had time to do all that and get back to make sure Cece made it to work.

She picked up the pile of unopened mail behind the front door and put it on the coffee table. The mess in the house was starting to chafe at her, the mess and the complete absence of any personality. No food, no decor. It was as if Cece didn't really live there.

It gave Julienne the creeps.

She knocked on Cece's door before she entered. Light streamed through the windows onto Cece's bed, and the room smelled like yesterday's Thai food.

"Ugh," Cece said.

"You said to wake you," Julienne said, hoping her voice sounded more confident than she felt. She still wasn't sure how she was supposed to make sure Cece kept up her obligations.

Cece cracked open one eye to look at her. Last night's makeup was smudged on her face and her pillow.

"How are you feeling?"

"I'm fine," Cece said. She swung her feet to the floor with a thump. "You sleep okay?"

"Good, thanks," Julienne said.

Cece caught sight of her reflection and scrunched up her nose. "Gross," she said.

Even hungover and barely awake, Julienne thought Cece looked far from gross. Cute, almost, if Julienne allowed her thoughts to go that far.

"Your coffee machine is broken," Julienne said.

"Oh, yeah, it is."

Cece didn't offer any other explanation.

The silence hung between them. It felt strangely intimate to see Cece like this, more vulnerable than she'd been before.

"I'm gonna get up," Cece said, gesturing vaguely at the room. Julienne took that as her cue to leave. She sat on her bed in the other room, scrolling on her phone. She waited until she heard the noise of the shower turning on before she relaxed.

This was her life, for the foreseeable future. She thought of the paycheck, and the freedom of not being dependent on her parents. She thought of the opportunities. It was worth the strange banality of it.

She heard the slide of the shower door and then a brief silence before Cece gently knocked on her door. Cece was wearing sweatpants and a loose t-shirt when she opened the door, her feet bare.

"Hey," Cece said, her voice soft. "Sorry about the lack of coffee. I usually swing by Starbucks on my way to set."

"We can do that," Julienne said.

Cece nodded. "Sorry about..." she gestured vaguely, "everything else, too."

Julienne shrugged.

Cece nodded, again, as if she'd done what she came here to do. It was the first time Julienne had seen her look awkward.

"Let me just grab some shoes and we can go," Cece said.

It wasn't long before they were in Cece's car, two iced coffees in the cupholder, and pulling up to set.

"What's the plan for today?" Julienne asked.

"I've got a few scenes to shoot," Cece said, checking something on her phone. "It'll be pretty boring, probably."

Julienne shrugged.

"You're even quieter today," Cece said. She flashed Julienne a smile. "I haven't scared you off, have I?"

"You're fine," Julienne said. "I just get hungry in the mornings."

Cece grinned at her. "Oh, if you want food, we can find you food. There's usually loads on set."

Cece took the lead, heading for a space past her own trailer where the catering was set up. "It's a bit early for the good lunch stuff, but I'm sure they'll have something."

"How come there's no food at your place?" Julienne asked.

Cece shrugged. "I don't like cooking," she said. "Plus I keep weird hours, so I just snack a lot."

"Your cupboards are basically empty," Julienne said. She grabbed a sandwich from the catering table.

"My trainer makes meals for me sometimes," Cece said. "I don't eat at home reliably enough for it to be worth keeping food there. I hate throwing it away."

Julienne took a bite of the sandwich, chewing it thoughtfully before she replied. "You're not great at looking after yourself."

Cece laughed. "Name a nineteen year old who is, Jules."

Julienne thought back to her own eating habits at nineteen, sharing a dorm room with Reina. Most of her food was cooked in the microwave or by someone else. "Fair point," she said.

"Don't worry about me," Cece said. She already looked taller, more confident than she had a few hours ago. "We made it here on time, didn't we?"

Julienne was amazed by her ability to bounce back.

Cece carried right on talking. "I have to go to hair and makeup, but you can hang out in my trailer if you want. Or you can like, go, I guess? There's not much for you to do today."

"No parties tonight?" Julienne asked.

"Nah," Cece said. "If you stick around a couple of hours I can give you a ride home or to the gym or wherever, or you can just get a cab. Sadie will probably pay for it."

"You sure you don't want me?" Julienne asked.

Cece rolled her eyes. "Seriously, there's nothing for you to be doing here. You're not missing anything."

"Tomorrow?"

Cece hummed, considering. "Come by my place around 10am."

"Alright," Julienne said. She got out her phone and ordered an Uber. There was no point waiting around, and she wanted to go home and shower and put on clean clothes. She could even go to the gym.

"I might even tidy up the house for you," Cece said, flashing Julienne a quick grin before she was met by someone brandishing some hairspray and ushered in another direction.

Julienne felt a little guilty, suddenly, for all the time she'd been judging Cece for having bare walls and unopened mail. She hadn't realised Cece could tell.

She got home and showered, said hi to Tori, grabbed her gym bag, and headed back out again. The gym session was long and intense, to make up for missing the previous day, and she relished the sweat on her brow and the burn in her muscles.

It was only mid-afternoon by the time she got home, and Tori had finished working on an article and moved to the living room, flicking through channels. Julienne settled on the couch beside her.

"You didn't come home last night," Tori said, shooting her a sly grin. "Good for you."

Julienne flushed. "It's the new job," Julienne said. "It has overnights, sometimes."

Tori raised her eyebrows. "Every time you mention this job it sounds even more suspicious."

Julienne hesitated. "I'm just a personal assistant," she said. "It's not a big deal."

"I have so many questions," Tori said.

"I signed an NDA."

"But you still let your new boss tag you in a photo?" Tori asked. She looked a little smug.

Julienne blinked. "I totally forgot about that. I muted all the notifications."

"I mean, there's no other way you'd be at a party with

Cece Browne," Tori said. "You should watch Bare Windows, it's really good."

"It feels weird to watch her on TV when I spent all day with her yesterday," Julienne said.

"She's really good in it," Tori said. "I bet she'll get a supporting actor nomination this year."

"I'll tell her you said that," Julienne said, half-joking. She didn't think her and Cece were in a place where Cece cared what her roommate thought of her. Not yet, anyway.

"Maybe you'll get to go to an awards show," Tori said.

Julienne pulled a face. "Let's not." She sighed. "I wish I could talk to you about it, to be honest. You're more used to brushing elbows with celebrities than I am."

"Ugh, don't remind me of that internship," Tori said.

"Sorry," Julienne said. "I'm gonna be around a bit less than usual, anyway."

"Bet you're excited to pay your own rent," Tori said.

Julienne nodded. "Thanks for putting up with me all this time," she said. "I owe you at least one dinner."

"At least one," Tori agreed. "Plus we should go out to celebrate, anyway."

Julienne smiled. "If Cece doesn't keep me too busy," she said.

Tori huffed a soft laugh. Julienne wasn't sure she really deserved a celebratory dinner. She barely understood how she got this job, and she had no real idea what she was doing.

The thought made her feel exhausted. She grabbed a snack from the cupboard and settled in for a quiet evening with Tori, the TV more background noise than anything else. She scrolled through her notifications on her phone, trying not to feel anxious about the new followers.

She had only been working with Cece for one day and she already felt wrung out, exhausted.

She had no idea what the rest of the week would bring.

TEN

The first thing Julienne saw when she woke up was a missed call from an unknown number, and a text from the same number.

"Hey, it's Cece. Just wanted to make sure you had my number :)" was timestamped at 3.37am.

Why the hell was Cece up so late, Julienne wondered, saving her number in her phone. That worried her even more than the missed call did. She'd set her alarm early enough that she'd have time to go to the gym before heading over to Cece's, but now she rushed through her morning routine and cut short her time in the gym. She stopped at Starbucks on the way, figuring if Cece was sleep deprived, she'd need all the help she could get, and got to Cece's half an hour earlier than agreed.

She rang the doorbell.

"It's open," Cece called from inside.

Julienne pushed the door open, wondering if Cece locked it at night. She added that to the mental list of concerns she had about Cece's wellbeing.

"Cece?" she said, looking around the foyer.

"I'm in here," Cece said. Her voice came from the living room.

Julienne stepped through the doorway and then stopped; she didn't know where to look first.

The mail that she'd stacked on the coffee table was now scattered in various piles, some envelopes torn open. The trash can had been moved to the centre of the room and was full of scraps of paper.

Cece sat cross-legged on the sofa. The blinds were drawn and the room was dark.

"What happened?" Julienne asked, flicking the light on. She crossed the room to lift the blinds and let the sunlight in.

Cece wrinkled her nose. "I sorted my mail," she said. She sounded exhausted. "It took hours."

"Have you slept?" Julienne asked.

She was sure Cece's iced coffee was growing warm in her hand, but she wasn't sure if she wanted Cece to have it. Worry started to nibble at her gut. Julienne was supposed to be the responsible adult in this situation, but she didn't know where to start.

"No," Cece said, her voice small. "I took an Adderall to help me get through it but then I couldn't sleep, so I just kept going."

Oh, god. Julienne had never been one for study drugs but she'd known a few people who'd taken Adderall when they had a deadline in college.

"How are you feeling?" she asked, her tone carefully neutral.

Cece scowled. "Like I've been awake for 24 hours straight."

"Have you eaten?"

Cece shook her head.

"We've got a bit of time," Julienne said, trying to keep her tone even. She had a feeling if she started freaking out, Cece would start being a dick about it.

She did not feel qualified for this.

"Do you want me to order you some breakfast? We can get it delivered here before you have to be on set." She tried to sound like this was normal, like this was a sensible thing to do right now.

Cece nodded. "You came early," she said.

Julienne bit her lip. "You texted me at 3am. I was worried."

Cece snorted. "Sounds about right."

Cece's iPad was on the coffee table, too, a crack in the screen protector, and Julienne sat down on the couch next to Cece to order. She tapped in something she thought sounded like a filling breakfast and got Cece's approval before ordering it.

"You really have your life together, huh," Cece said, sounding a little annoyed by it.

"No, I really don't," Julienne said. She thought of the months she'd spent doing nothing in her apartment, the phone calls to her parents that she hadn't made.

"I bet you regret taking this job," Cece said, her tone a little sharp.

Julienne tensed. "I started two days ago," she said. "I'm still getting used to this."

"I could see you judging me yesterday," Cece said. "I wanted to make my house less of a fucking mess."

"I wasn't judging," Julienne said. Her heart thudded a little in her chest.

Cece rolled her eyes. "Don't lie to me, c'mon. I'm being honest with you." She leaned back on the couch and shut her eyes. "I'm so tired, man."

"I bought you a coffee," Julienne said. "I don't know if that's a good idea."

Cece shook a hand dismissively. "It'll be fine," she said, picking up the cup and taking a sip.

A small smile appeared on her face. "You remembered my order."

"My friend Reina has the most complicated order, yours is pretty easy," Julienne said.

They lapsed into silence as they waited for Cece's breakfast to arrive. Julienne started to tidy up the mess Cece had made, with a little direction from Cece, who sprawled out as she watched.

"I can't believe I have to go to work," Cece said.

Julienne didn't say anything as she brought some semblance of order to the living room. She wasn't sure what kind of system Cece had come up with to sort her mail, so she didn't try to disrupt any of the piles.

"It feels like you're judging me now," Cece said.

Julienne stopped tidying and looked at her. "Are you trying to pick a fight?"

"Yes. No. I don't know," Cece said. She sighed.

"I'm just trying to help," Julienne said gently. "That's my job. Helping you."

"Right," Cece said. "Right."

Julienne shrugged. "Next time, instead of taking Adderall on a work night, you could just call me."

"Really?" Cece said. "That's so needy, though. I'd hate me for doing that."

The doorbell rang, saving Julienne from answering. She collected the burger and fries she'd ordered for Cece's breakfast and put on a plate for Cece.

"I'm not going to do it all on my own while you do nothing," Julienne said. "But if we did it together instead of you staying up all night when you have to work, that'd be okay."

Cece bit her lip. "Sorry," she said. She started picking at the fries.

Julienne didn't know what to say to that.

"God, I'm such a fuckup," Cece said. "Sam is going to be so mad."

"You can still go to work," Julienne said.

"I will but I'll be useless. I'm so tired I can't think straight. And, no offense, but nearly everything you say makes me want to fight you."

Julienne swallowed. That was not encouraging to hear.

Cece carried on talking as she chewed. "God, do not let me shittalk Sam to his face," she said. "I will actually lose my job."

Julienne took a deep breath. "I won't let that happen," she said. She had no idea how she was going to keep that promise.

Cece took a bite of the burger. She chewed it over slowly, considering something, and sauce dripped down her chin.

Julienne checked the time. They needed to leave soon, and she wasn't sure Cece was going to arrive on set ready to work at all.

"Let's just go," Cece said. "I can eat in the car."

"You want me to drive?" Julienne asked.

Cece shrugged. "Sure," she said.

Julienne felt a little embarrassed that Cece Browne would be sitting in her car. She probably owned clothes more expensive than Julienne's car.

Cece didn't comment on it, though, when she got in, and she focused on her food for most of the journey. The only conversation was Julienne asking for directions.

"I really am just trying to help," Julienne said, as they pulled into the parking lot.

Cece offered Julienne her remaining fries. "Peace offering," she said. "I'm an asshole when I'm coming down."

"I think you need those more than I do," Julienne said.

Cece laughed. "You're probably right. You ever taken any Adderall?"

Julienne shook her head. "Drugs aren't really my thing."

"Fair," Cece said. She finished off the fries and opened the car door. "Let's get this over with."

Julienne took a deep breath and followed. For once, Cece wasn't paces ahead of her. They dropped some of Cece's stuff at her trailer first and then went to hair and makeup.

"I know, I look like shit," Cece said, before the makeup artist had a chance to say anything. "This is Julienne, I don't think I introduced you the other day."

"Nice to meet you," the makeup artist said. "I'm Lily."

Julienne smiled at her.

"Do you want some water or anything?" Julienne asked Cece.

"Nah, I'm good," Cece said.

"You can sit down if you want," Lily said. "I remember being a PA, always on my feet."

"Thanks," Julienne said, taking a seat next to Cece.

Cece didn't say anything as Lily started to work on her face, softly tutting as she covered her dark circles.

"You stayed up too late," Lily said.

Cece glanced at Julienne. "You are not the first person to tell me that."

"Don't I know it," Lily said.

Julienne watched in silence as Lily transformed Cece's face into someone who looked a little younger, a little softer round the edges. The makeup was thick for the harsh lighting.

"You're early," Sam said, appearing around the corner.

"I'm not feeling great," Cece said. "Just to warn you."

Sam sucked air through his teeth. "What kind of not feeling great?"

Julienne felt like she could see the cogs turning in Cece's head. "I didn't get much sleep," she said. "Just a little tired and rundown."

"Well, you're here, at least," Sam said, though he didn't look happy about it. "Drink some coffee, get into character. We've got a busy day today."

Cece jokingly saluted him and Sam rolled his eyes and walked off.

"This is going to suck," Cece said.

"Everyone has off days," Julienne said. "Just gotta get through a few hours and then you can go home and go to bed."

Cece grunted in response.

Julienne had no idea how to give an effective pep talk. She was used to tennis matches and consoling her roommate after a shitty day at work. This was another world entirely.

"All done," Lily said. "Go get dressed, gorgeous."

Cece flashed her a winning grin. Julienne accompanied Cece over to wardrobe, and averted her eyes as Cece got dressed.

"Are you gonna stay and watch?" Cece asked Julienne. Her eyes were a little wide, making her look oddly vulnerable. Maybe it was the makeup, turning her into someone's teenage daughter.

"Sure," Julienne said.

"It helps," Cece said. At Julienne's confused look, she elaborated: "to know you're looking out for me."

"That's what I'm here for," Julienne said, but she couldn't help but feel a little warm at Cece's affection.

Cece sat in a chair with someone else's name on it, told Julienne to sit in her own, and thumbed through the script. Her leg bounced in the chair and she fidgeted, and Julienne wondered if everyone else was tracking those moves and could tell that Cece was coming down from something.

She needed this job and she needed Cece functioning for that.

The director beckoned Cece over and Julienne felt a hard knot of anxiety form in her stomach.

She watched as the scene began. Cece was working alongside another young actor, someone Julienne vaguely recognised but couldn't name. She guessed that they were playing siblings, and suddenly wished that she'd asked Tori more questions about the show so she wouldn't feel so lost.

She could tell, though, that Cece wasn't acting as well as she had on Monday. She forgot her line more than once, and even Julienne could see that her movements seemed a little stiff.

Julienne bit her lip. It was making her more anxious to watch, but she didn't want to abandon Cece.

The director stepped into the scene to intervene, and there was a discussion Julienne couldn't hear. She could read the body language that he wasn't happy, though, and Cece looked like she wanted to argue.

They tried again. And again. And again.

Julienne didn't know how she could help.

Cece mistakes seemed to be getting worse. In one take, she started using lines from a completely different scene. In another, she completely zoned out and missed her cue.

Cece asked for a five minute break and approached Julienne.

"Can we take a walk?" she said. "I need some fresh air or something."

"Sure," Julienne said, falling into step beside her.

"I'm really fucking this up," Cece said, her voice gravelly with exhaustion.

Julienne tried to stay positive. "It's just one bad day," she said. "There will be other, better days."

"You heard Sam's warning," Cece said. "If I lose this job I'll be a joke."

"What have you done before when you feel like crap?"

"I don't show up," Cece said.

"Oh," Julienne said.

Cece frowned. "There's a reason Sadie had to hire a babysitter."

"She said it was a strategy you agreed to," Julienne said. She was trying to choose her words carefully, but it was hard to figure out what Cece was thinking.

"Well, yeah," Cece said. Her tone turned a little ugly. "I can't even open my own mail without fucking it up. I can't do anything on my own."

Julienne swallowed. "You're trying," she said softly. "Sometimes it takes practice to get it right."

"Screw ups still have consequences, though." Cece said.

Julienne wasn't sure if Cece was still talking about what she was facing today or something else, but she stuck with it. "Today is just a few hours of your life and then you can go home and sleep for as long as you need. You just need one good take."

Cece squared her shoulders a little and nodded. The loop they were walking was coming back around to the entrance of the building.

"You're always so reasonable," Cece said. She sounded a little annoyed by it, which was true to form.

"I'm the reliable, boring friend," Julienne said.

"I don't mind boring," Cece said, giving Julienne a small smile.

Julienne didn't know what to say to that. She changed tack: "Maybe if you decorated your place it'd feel more like home," she said. "You'd want to look after it."

Cece gave a contemplative hum as they entered the building. "I'll think about it," she said.

At the edge of the set, Sam was waiting, arms folded and a stern expression on his face. Julienne linked her arm with Cece to reassure her as they approached him.

"You can't just go walkabout," Sam said. "You are already putting production behind."

"I asked for a five minute break," Cece said. "I needed to get my head together."

Sam's lip curled. "This is your last warning, Cece. Get it together or you leave the show. We don't have time for your bullshit."

Cece closed her mouth with a click and her cheeks flushed red. Julienne wanted to give her a hug.

Sam turned his attention to her. "You're meant to be keeping her in line," he said, his voice a frustrated growl.

"I'm not a prison warden," Julienne said. "She's here and she's trying."

Sam made a disparaging sound. "If the two of you cost me overtime today..." he trailed off, leaving the threat hanging in the air, and turned on his heel and walked away.

Cece stared after him, looking a little pale.

Julienne reached down and squeezed her hand. "You can do this, Cece."

"He's such an asshole," she muttered.

"Tell me about this scene," Julienne said, trying to focus on the task at hand.

Cece furrowed her brow. She dropped Julienne's hand and grabbed a script from a nearby table.

Julienne missed the contact immediately, and that thought sent heat to her cheeks.

She didn't know how to get used to being close to Cece like that.

She was only half-listening while Cece explained the scene to her, but as Cece spoke she could see her head getting more in it.

"You got this," she said, when Cece finished. She tried to inject all the positive energy she'd give out to a teammate before a tennis match into her words.

Cece gave her a curt nod and stepped away from the conversation. She stretched, contorting her body, before stepping in front of the camera.

Cece made eye contact with her for just a beat before the cameras were rolling, and Julienne felt her cheeks heat up a little. She wondered if anyone else noticed.

She really wanted Cece to do well. Not just for the sake of her job, but because she was starting to really like Cece.

She tried to ignore the twist in her gut at that realization.

Just as a friend, she told herself.

ELEVEN

Shooting for the rest of the day was still a little painful, but Cece's head was more in it and eventually the director was satisfied he got the take he needed. To Julienne's relief, Sam's office door stayed closed throughout.

Julienne was a little proud of Cece pulling it together enough to finish on time. This job, keeping Cece in line, it was all starting to feel like her new normal.

She gave Cece a ride home and spent a quiet evening watching a documentary. Even though her routine had been turned on its head, it was nice to keep some old habits, and documentaries made her brain work in a completely different way to working with Cece. She got an early night, went to the gym early the next morning, and then headed over to Cece's.

"I should get you a key," Cece said, as she let Julienne in. "To really maximise your ability to yell at me when I sleep in."

Julienne laughed. "You're in a better mood."

"I slept so well," Cece said. "Let's go out for breakfast?"

Julienne nodded and followed Cece to her car, which

gleamed in the morning sun.

Cece drove them to a diner a few blocks from her house, and Julienne wondered if they could have walked and enjoyed the sun a little. She didn't know West Hollywood well, and she loved exploring different parts of LA, seeing what they had to offer. The city was teeming with culture, and she wanted to explore Cece's world.

They found a table tucked away in the corner and ordered. Julienne ordered a three egg omelette and Cece got the pancake special, not even asking what it was.

Cece sipped her coffee and wrinkled her nose. "The only bad thing about this place is they don't do iced coffee."

"What's the plan today?" Julienne asked.

For the first time, Cece looked a little shy. "I have a favour to ask you, actually."

"What's up?"

"My place sucks," she said. "You know it, I know it. I never invite anyone around because I kind of hate it. I haven't decorated it at all."

"Do you want to go shopping?" Julienne asked. "I don't know where you'd go around here but I'm sure we can find something."

Cece nodded, biting her lip. "I just don't really know where to start."

"How long have you lived there?"

Cece shrugged. "Since we started filming Bare Windows, so like... nearly two years, I guess?"

"You didn't bring stuff from your old place?"

Cece twisted her mouth, looking unsure of herself. "I threw out a lot of stuff. Sold some of it on eBay. After my mom died I just wanted to get rid of everything, start fresh."

"Sorry about your mum," Julienne said.

"Thanks," Cece said. "It's not like, a big deal. I just felt like I owed my whole career to her, y'know? I needed to figure out who I was without her."

"Have you?" Julienne asked.

"Huh?"

"Have you figured out who you are?" she said. The question felt a little silly when she said the whole thing.

Cece hummed, thinking about it. "I don't know." She paused. "I wish I hadn't sold everything, though. I couldn't look at my first award without thinking about how proud she was that night, so I sold it to a fan. It's probably gone forever, now."

"That sounds really hard," Julienne said.

"Yeah," Cece said. She paused again, then waved a hand dismissively. "Whatever, it's done now. It's been years."

"How old were you when she died?"

"Fifteen," Cece said. She looked at Julienne over her coffee cup and she looked so small and vulnerable. If they weren't in a diner she would have given Cece a hug right then.

Their food arrived, steaming hot and smelling delicious. Cece dug into her pancakes and Julienne decided it was time to change the subject.

"So what kind of vibe do you want to go for in your condo?"

Cece chewed thoughtfully. "I want it to be peaceful. Just nice and calming. I texted my landlady and she said it's fine if I want to paint, so long as it's not a mess."

Cece cleared her throat. "You don't have to paint with me, though," she said quickly. "I know it's a lot to ask."

Julienne shrugged. "We might not fit all of it in today," she said. "But we can make a plan once we've gone shopping, make it work with your schedule."

"You should be an events planner," Cece said. "When you're done with me, I mean. You're so organised."

Julienne laughed. "I just like the future being predictable. I think I'm the opposite of you."

"Makes us a good team," Cece said.

Even though her tone was casual, Cece's words made warmth boom in Julienne's chest. She liked being on Cece's team.

More than she probably should.

She focused on her omelette instead of conversation, and then they headed out. Cece passed Julienne her phone with a map already open on it and asked her to direct. Julienne had never heard of the place they were going.

"I asked Joshua where we should go," Cece explained. "He knows about like, aesthetics and stuff."

"I only really shop in Ikea," Julienne said, feeling a little sheepish.

Cece parked the car. "If you fall in love with something here, just say. I'll buy it for you!"

Julienne blinked. She wondered, for a second, if Cece pitied her, but one glance at Cece's brilliant smile won her over. She grabbed a shopping cart and followed Cece into the store.

"What are you looking for?" she asked.

Cece shrugged. "Maybe like, a wall hanging or something? I was thinking blues and greens."

Julienne hummed. Cece seemed to flit about the store, easily distracted by ideas before discarding them.

"What's your place look like?" Cece asked.

Julienne bit her lip. "It's just an apartment I share with a friend from college," she said. "We haven't done much to it, really."

"Helpful," Cece said. She stuck her tongue out at

Julienne.

Julienne shrugged. "Our landlord isn't as forgiving as yours. We've made it pretty cosy, though."

"Are you from California? You've never said."

She nodded. "I was born in SoCal, but we moved to England when I was 11 and stayed there till I came back for college. My mum is English."

"That's very cool," Cece said. "You kept that so quiet, if I'd lived in Europe I would never shut up about it." She picked up a cushion, thought about it, and put it back.

"It wasn't like, London or anywhere glamorous. Just a small town where it always rained." She sighed. "If I didn't get this job I probably would have to move back," Julienne admitted. She didn't know why she was telling Cece any of this. That wasn't part of her job description, but something about Cece made her want to open up and tell her everything.

"And then you wouldn't have ever met me," Cece said, grinning at her.

Julienne laughed.

"Shame you have an American accent," Cece continued. "English accents are awesome."

Julienne shrugged. "I guess I'm one of those people whose accent was set in stone pretty early," she said. "I've always been bad at languages, too."

"My Spanish is pretty bad," Cece said. "My mom was Mexican American, so that's pretty embarrassing."

"You didn't speak Spanish at home?"

Cece shrugged. "I don't think her Spanish was that great either. Maybe if we'd stayed in touch with her family after we moved to LA."

"What about your dad?" Julienne asked, gently.

"Never met him," Cece said. "He dipped before I was

born. He wasn't hispanic, though, if that's what you're asking."

"I don't know what I was asking," Julienne said, truthfully. She'd just wanted to know more about Cece, as if maybe that would explain why she was the way she was.

Cece shrugged and kept walking. They turned a corner and found all the mocked up living spaces. It was definitely higher end than Ikea, and when Julienne checked a price-tag she winced.

Cece hummed as she browsed, a tune that Julienne couldn't place but was comforting regardless.

"You're not normally indecisive," Julienne said.

Cece bit her lip. "I've put off decorating for so long," she said. "I'm only gonna do it once, right? So it has to be right."

"We can just return it and try again," Julienne reminded her.

"It's taken me a year to get to the store once, you think I'm gonna get here twice?"

Julienne laughed.

"Maybe I should just give up on this and get a cat," Cece said. "A cat makes a place a home faster than decorating."

"Or we could not give up," Julienne said.

"You pick something."

"It's your home," she said. "It needs to be right for you, not me."

Cece groaned.

Julienne changed tack. "Why don't you tell me what you do and don't like about this one?" Julienne said, pointing at the set up that had an expensive-looking beach aesthetic.

"It looks a bit too polished," Cece said. "Like a set for a photoshoot, not somewhere you live."

Julienne paused. "Maybe something a bit more rustic?"

Cece pulled a face. "I hate that word, rustic."

"I don't really know what to suggest. Maybe you should have brought Joshua, instead."

"Aw, babe, you're doing fine," Cece said, and Julienne wondered if it was normal that she got goosebumps when Cece called her babe.

"Why don't we just look at some of the art they have," Julienne said. "Instead of a whole set up."

Cece nodded. "Maybe all I need is one amazing, show-stopping, brilliant work of art, and that'll solve all of my problems."

"Maybe," Julienne said uncertainly.

Cece looked around and found a salesperson and approached them to ask for help, and they were directed to a section of the store where all the bigger art pieces were.

"You're right, this is better," Cece said as they approached.

There were a few paintings and prints hung on the walls and Julienne tried not to pull a face at the hefty price tags dangling from their frames. There were a few more in a rack, and Cece rifled through those first before stepping back to look at the wall.

"I like that one," she said, pointing to a painting of a woman swimming in the ocean. "It's really pretty. The blue is the same colour as your eyes."

Julienne's breath caught in her throat. She didn't know what to say to that. She didn't even know where to file that in her brain.

"Thanks," she croaked out.

"I'm going to go get someone to help us get it down," Cece said, apparently unaware of the effect she'd had on Julienne.

Her face felt hot and her heart thudded in her chest. She tried to gather herself before Cece returned, so she wasn't standing stupefied in the aisle, thinking about when Cece had noticed the colour of her eyes.

Cece was back quickly, bouncing on her heels as the sales clerk accompanied her and she pointed out the painting. He wrapped it up and took it to the cash register for her, and Cece's mood seemed to have lifted completely. She was decisive, picking up cushions, a fabric wall hanging, and a rug, and tossing them into the cart.

"We just need some paint," Cece said, grinning.

"How are you going to hang those up?" Julienne asked.

Cece pointed a finger at her. "I'd be lost without you," she said, sounding sincere. "We should go to a DIY store, it'll be cheaper than here, and we can get the paint too."

"I didn't realise you were on a budget," Julienne said, only half joking.

Cece raised an eyebrow at her and Julienne just shrugged in response. She didn't know when they became able to communicate without words, but it made her heart beat a little faster if she let herself think about it.

They checked out, Julienne trying not to pull a face at the price and the blasé way Cece whipped out her card to pay for it, and got someone to help them load up the car before driving on to the next place.

"This has been fun, hasn't it?" Cece said, pulling into the parking lot.

"It has, yeah," Julienne said, and Cece hit her with a rare megawatt smile, and she thought if they hadn't been in the car she might have been weak at the knees.

Cece's smile was going to get her into trouble soon, if it hadn't already.

TWELVE

Cece took the wall hanging with her into the hardware store to help her pick out the paint colour. She didn't take long to make a decision, and Julienne picked up the rest of the stuff they needed while the paint was being mixed. She wondered what it was like to have a space that was all your own, to do with as you pleased. She liked living with Tori, but she'd love to have the freedom to decorate a whole apartment, to make that space all hers. She'd daydreamed about the kind of art she'd put on the walls, the houseplants she'd carefully nurture.

It was another way Cece's world was so different from her own. She could just do things, instead of daydreaming about them.

She met Cece at the checkout with all the hooks and fastenings she thought they'd need. It felt like they were barely in there for ten minutes.

"I guess we need to paint the walls first," Cece said, loading rollers and trays into the trunk of her car.

"I am amazed you can fit all that into your car," Julienne said.

Cece shrugged. "I used to keep my entire life in here, half my wardrobe, some snacks, a laptop. Sadie made me clean it out."

Julienne bit the inside of her cheek from smiling. She'd done that, too, with her first car.

It took two trips to unload everything once they got back to Cece's, and Julienne was surprised by how much of the day had disappeared. Time with Cece always seemed to go quicker than usual.

Cece looked at the pile of supplies and bit her lip. "It seems like a lot," she said, looking uncertain. "I don't know where to start."

"Do you know where you want to paint?"

Cece blinked at Julienne, as if she'd forgotten she was there. "Oh," she said. "I was thinking the wall behind the couch and the wall behind my bed. Like a statement wall thing."

Julienne hummed and tied her hair up while she tried to think. Soon, she'd made a plan for clearing the living room, covering the furniture, and protecting the fittings. It seemed like all Cece needed was a little push in the right direction and she threw all of her considerable enthusiasm into the task. In almost no time, the edges were taped up and the room was ready, and Julienne opened the windows while Cece searched for the perfect playlist to accompany them.

The sun was low in the sky and gentle pop music played through the speakers and Julienne wondered how this was her job, her life.

Cece opened the paint tin and poured it into the tray. She passed Julienne a roller, and it was easy to forget in the moment that Cece was her boss and not her friend. They started to paint, rolling broad strokes of a soft grey blue onto the wall.

The time passed quickly as they painted, talking about nothing in particular. It was dark outside by the time the first coat was finished, and Cece dropped her roller into a tray and slumped on the couch.

"You make it all seem so easy," she said. "I'd been ignoring this for so long."

"Some stuff is easier to ignore," Julienne said. She paused. "It took me a week to open an email from my parents. I knew they were going to make me move home."

"Just a week, though. This has been... months."

Julienne shrugged. "You're a busy person. I was unemployed, all I did was refresh my email all day."

"Maybe I should become a home decorator," Cece said. "That would make me get my life together."

Julienne raised an eyebrow. "You don't want to be an actress?"

Cece sighed. "I used to love it," she said. "Mom set everything up for me and made it happen, and I guess I was good at it. It used to feel like it was more her dream than mine, y'know? I just wanted to make her happy."

"You like working on Bare Windows, though," Julienne said.

Cece nodded. "It's a great show, and the critical acclaim doesn't hurt. I don't like all the attention, though. Sometimes I just want to be myself, by myself."

Julienne felt like their lives couldn't be any more different. Here she was, desperate to stay in LA where her friends were, putting her dreams on hold to take this job, and Cece had all the money in the world and no direction at all.

"Everyone always expects so much from me," Cece said,

wrapping her arms around her knees. "All I ever do is disappoint."

"What would you do if nobody else mattered?" Julienne asked.

Cece frowned, then shook her head. "Nothing, I guess."

"Come on," Julienne said. "What's your ideal day look like, how do you spend it?"

"I don't know," Cece said. She sounded frustrated, for the first time that day. "Do you know what you'd do?"

"I'd love to manage an art gallery," Julienne said. She remembered the sting of rejection from the week before, and it still hurt a little to think about. Who was she to have a dream like that?

"That sounds cool," Cece said, bringing her out of her thoughts.

Julienne shrugged. "It's just a dream, anyways. It's probably never gonna happen."

"Must be nice to have a goal you're working towards," Cece said, wistfully.

"You don't have to know what you want," Julienne said.

"What would you do, if you were me?"

"I'd be a terrible actor," Julienne said. "Nobody would have brought me to Hollywood as a kid."

Cece laughed.

"It's easy to see you're talented," Julienne continued. "I've barely been on set and I've seen it."

She wanted to tell Cece she couldn't take her eyes off her, but she wasn't quite brave enough to voice that thought.

"Thanks," Cece said. "You're paid to be here, though, so you kinda have to say that."

"Didn't I just say I'm a terrible actor?" Julienne said.

Cece stuck her tongue out and Julienne laughed.

The conversation drifted, and they started talking about

all the various projects that Cece had been considering. She hoped to do another movie when the next season of Bare Windows wrapped, but she hadn't signed on to anything yet, and Sadie was pushing her to make a decision.

"I'd love to do something gay," Cece said. "One day, maybe. I'm not sure I'm ready yet."

Julienne blinked. She'd suspected, but it was something else to have Cece confirm it. "I didn't know you were..." she trailed off.

"Yeah, I'm a lesbian," Cece said. "I'm not like, out-out, but all my friends know. Sadie thinks I should just come out, but it's complicated."

"It's always complicated," Julienne said. She paused. Then: "I'm bi, by the way."

Cece held out her hand to do a fist bump and Julienne obliged, tapping their knuckles together.

"I just want to do it right, y'know?" Cece said.

Julienne didn't know if Cece was talking about coming out, or the bad press, or something else entirely. She nodded anyway.

Cece sighed.

"It's getting kind of late," Julienne said. She checked the time on her phone. "I should head home."

"Yeah, of course," Cece said. "We'll do the bedroom tomorrow, and then you can come to Joshua's party with me."

"What time do you want me?"

Cece pulled a face. "Not too early," she said. "Oh, bring an overnight bag."

"Any idea what I should wear for this party?" Julienne asked.

Cece hummed. "I like dressing you up," she said. She smirked at Julienne.

Whatever Julienne had been planning to say died in her throat. Her heart skipped a beat.

Cece carried on talking. "Joshua is pretty flamboyant, so wear something with a bit of drama. I can find you something if you get stuck."

"Okay," Julienne said, unable to form a real sentence. All thought had left her brain.

Cece raised an eyebrow at her and she suddenly felt caught, like Cece knew exactly the effect her words were having on her.

"See you tomorrow," she said, and left as quickly as she could.

She spent the whole drive home thinking about Cece's smirk.

Tori was washing dishes when she got home and Julienne sat rigidly on the sofa, unable to relax.

"You okay?" Tori asked, dish towel in hand.

Julienne bit her lip. "You won't judge me, will you?"

"Never," Tori said.

Julienne sighed. "Have you ever had feelings for someone you work for?"

"Oh, shit," Tori said. She put the towel on the counter and came to sit beside her. "Cece Browne?"

Julienne nodded, burying her face in her hands.

"It's not the end of the world," Tori said. "She's pretty."

"I need this job, Tori."

"I know," Tori said. "Try to focus on the job. Have boundaries. You're great at boundaries."

Julienne thought boundaries might undo the progress she'd made with Cece so far. Her job was to help her. Either way she looked at it, she was screwed.

"I'm going to bed," she said.

Tori gave her a sympathetic smile and said goodnight.

From her bedroom, the quiet noise of Tori watching TV was almost comforting. She didn't know how long she lay awake, staring at the ceiling, thinking about the warmth that rose in her cheeks whenever Cece looked at her like that.

Cece was troubled, confrontational, erratic, and taming her was Julienne's only shot at staying in LA.

She needed Cece. The problem was, she wanted her too.

THIRTEEN

Julienne woke up early and went to the gym, trying not to think too much about yet another day in close quarters with Cece. The gym helped, it always did. It made her feel like she could handle anything.

She packed an overnight bag with a few outfits for the party. She'd gone out with the arts clique in college, so she had an idea of what dramatic outfits were, but she was pretty sure her info was out of date. She only agonised over them a little before making the decision to take all three options.

She wanted to impress Cece. She hated that she wanted to impress Cece.

She could hear music playing as she approached Cece's front door and pressed the doorbell. She hoped that meant Cece was in a good mood, and ready to face the day.

Cece opened the door. "Hey!" she said brightly. She tossed Julienne something and Julienne caught it without thinking, the sharp edge digging into her palm. "I found you a key!"

"Thanks," Julienne said. The key felt warm in her hand,

and she couldn't help but wonder if it meant something, that Cece trusted her enough to grant her access like that. No, she thought, it must just be a convenience thing. She couldn't let herself think it was anything more than that.

"I put up the tapestry upstairs, come see," Cece said, stepping aside so Julienne could enter.

Julienne followed Cece upstairs. It was amazing how much the hallway seemed different with just one change. It made it feel like a home, and the cool blues made the house seem very tranquil.

It *was* slightly lopsided, though.

"It looks great," Julienne said. "I think that corner needs moving."

"Yeah, it was hard to get it straight on my own," Cece said. Then: "Probably 'cause I'm gay."

Julienne snorted and Cece gave her a bright smile. She seemed more relaxed than Julienne had ever seen her.

"I'll climb on the chair and you tell me when it looks good," Cece said, moving the chair closer to the corner that needed moving.

She moved the hook on the wall slightly higher and refixed it, and then looked back to Julienne for approval.

"Perfect," she said.

Cece jumped down from the chair with a thud and stumbled, almost falling into Julienne. Julienne's breath caught in her throat as Cece caught herself, inches from her.

Cece grinned at her. "I'm all good," she said, and walked into her bedroom, and Julienne wondered if she was doing it on purpose. That thought hurt, a little, with all the possibility wrapped in it.

She shook herself and followed Cece. She couldn't let herself obsess over every small contact she had with her. They spent a little time moving and covering the furniture and taping up the edges of the wall, and the feeling of having a task to do was a pleasant distraction. She set up the paint in the trays and soon they were ready to go. Julienne had always liked being busy, having a goal to work towards and a plan to get there. It helped her cope when feelings got complicated.

And Cece definitely made things complicated.

Julienne rolled a stripe of paint onto the wall. "I checked your calendar," she said, "and I was wondering why you always party when you have work the next day."

"I don't dictate the LA nightlife, it just happens that way," Cece said. "But tonight is Joshua's birthday thing, I wouldn't miss it for the world."

"Did you get him a present?"

"I booked a gay stripper."

Julienne swallowed. She didn't know what to say to that.

"I didn't," Cece said. Julienne could hear the smile in her voice. "Just wanted to see the look on your face."

Julienne took her eyes off the wall to look at Cece, who was grinning at her.

"I'm not a prude," Julienne said.

Cece raised an eyebrow at her. "Sure," she said, still wearing a small smile.

For a brief moment, Julienne wanted to kiss that smug look off her face.

God, she was in trouble.

She focused on painting, sometimes humming along to the pop music in the background. The bedroom was smaller than the living room, and they finished quickly, moving all of their painting stuff downstairs to do a second coat on that wall.

They worked from the outside edges towards the

middle, nearly tripping over each other as they were close to finishing up. It wasn't helped by Cece dancing along to the music, waving her roller around. She knocked into Julienne and threw her off balance, and her roller landed a great splat of paint on Cece's arm.

Cece laughed, a lovely bright sound that Julienne wanted to hear again and again and again.

"Sorry," she said.

Cece shrugged, still grinning, then looked at her roller.

"Oh no," Julienne said, and Cece darted forward, waving her paint covered roller in Julienne's face in a threatening manner.

Soon, she had Julienne backed up against the sofa. She crowded in close, and suddenly all Julienne could hear was the sound of both of them breathing. She could feel Cece's body heat as their arms brushed, and it felt like time stopped for a second and she gazed into Cece's intense brown eyes. Her gaze dropped to Cece's lips, just for one, dangerous moment before she caught herself.

Heat rushed to her face. She was certain her cheeks were bright red.

Cece tapped the damp roller lightly on the tip of Julienne's nose and stepped away.

Julienne exhaled shakily.

"Revenge," Cece said. She tossed the roller in the tray and turned to the kitchen sink to wash the paint off her arm.

Julienne exhaled.

"Can you help me hang the painting up?" Cece said. "I tried doing it on my own but I got stuck."

"Sure," Julienne said, trying to control her voice.

Maybe it was best if she didn't speak. Her brain seemed to turn to mush whenever Cece invaded her personal space.

Forming sentences when she could count the freckles on her cheeks was an impossible task.

Getting the painting on the wall wasn't difficult; Cece just needed a second pair of eyes. When they were finished, Cece seemed to be at a loose end, unsure of what to do.

"We've got a few hours to kill," Cece said. "Joshua hates it when people arrive early."

"Does anyone in LA arrive early?" Julienne asked.

Cece shrugged. She hit a button on her phone and the music paused.

"We could watch a movie," Julienne said.

Cece twisted her mouth, looking around the living room, still in disarray. "It stinks of paint in here. Let's go out and do something instead."

Julienne worried at her lip. Her instinct was to stay and reorder the living room, but she didn't want to push Cece.

"Where do you want to go?" Julienne asked.

"Dunno," Cece said. "Where do you want to go? We always do what I want to do."

Julienne laughed. "You're literally the boss here, Cece."

Cece pursed her lips. "I'm not *your* boss. That's Sadie's job. I'm not responsible."

"Nobody would mistake you for responsible," Julienne said.

Cece blinked at her and then burst into peals of laughter. "You have the best sense of humour," she said. "What do you like doing when you're not at the gym? Art galleries, right?"

"I do," Julienne said. "But we don't have to go to one, you'll be bored."

She had a feeling that Cece would be like Reina in an art gallery, flitting around and enjoying herself for the first half an hour and then bored to death while Julienne considered each work of art carefully for another two hours. Julienne usually planned for an entire day to spend in a gallery, not just an afternoon before moving on to something else. It took time to really appreciate art, in her opinion.

"I can like art," Cece said.

"I like to take my time at art galleries, we've only got a few hours."

Cece hummed. "What's the middle ground between an art gallery and something I would want to do?"

"A party at an art gallery?"

"Hah, we should definitely go to one of those one day," Cece said. "I can get drunk and you can explain all the hidden meanings behind the art."

Julienne laughed. "That does sound fun," she said. She wasn't sure what it meant that Cece was talking about a *one day* for the two of them, as if they were in each other's lives now.

Or maybe she just meant another day.

"Let's go to a bookstore," Cece said, drawing Julienne out of her thoughts.

"You read?"

"I'm not an idiot," Cece said, sounding a little affronted.

"There aren't any books here, that's all," Julienne said.

"I keep some in my trailer. There's usually a lot of downtime on set."

"Sure, okay, let's go to a bookstore," Julienne said, and grabbed her handbag where she'd left it by the door.

"Um, Jules," Cece said, still standing in the living room looking at her. A smile was tugging at her lips.

"What's up?"

Cece looked like she was holding in a laugh. "You've still got paint on your nose, babe."

Julienne's face heated up and she darted to the bathroom to wash her face. The paint had dried on her nose, and she had to rub at it till it was raw to get it off. Her face was left a splotchy red, and she grimaced at her reflection, her bangs hanging damp and limp over her forehead.

She took a deep breath. Were her eyes really the same shade of blue as that painting? They stood out even more against her flushed skin.

She exhaled upwards, ruffling her bangs, and then ran her fingers through her hair, trying to get it to sit right. She hoped she didn't look like the disaster she felt like.

Cece was just so distracting, all the time. Julienne almost lost track of herself when she was around her; she just wanted to focus on Cece. She was magnetic.

"I'll drive," Cece said, when Julienne rejoined her at the front door. "We can get some takeout on the way home."

Cece pulled out into the road and passed Julienne her phone to pick some music for the short journey.

"Hey," Cece said. "Thanks for today. I wouldn't have done it without you."

Julienne smiled. "No problem," she said.

Cece reached over and gave her knee a gentle squeeze. "I mean it," she said.

And then the moment was over and she was pulling into the underground parking lot. They rode the lift into the store and once they stepped out Julienne took a moment to appreciate the size of the store.

"I forgot how big this place was," she said, looking down from the mezzanine at the four floors below her.

"Mom used to come here a lot when I was a kid," Cece said. "She loved to read, loved to try and guess what would be adapted to film."

Julienne smiled. "I brought my dad here when he came to visit in junior year."

Cece ran her finger along a shelf full of fantasy books. "He came all the way here from England?"

"He sometimes has business here," Julienne said. "He only moved to England for my mum. My gran got sick and she had to care for her."

She didn't know why she was telling Cece this. She didn't think Cece would care.

"Your parents are still together?" Cece asked.

"Yeah, twenty-six years." Julienne said. She didn't know what else to say. The silence that settled over them felt a little awkward. "I'm gonna go browse," she said, gesturing pointlessly.

Cece nodded.

Julienne wished she was more charismatic, outgoing. She wished she could get Cece to open up. She just walked away instead, finding herself thumbing through a book on display, not really taking any of it in.

She put it back on the display and straightened the stack of books before she left it. Nothing nearby seemed to be really grabbing her, so she turned around to find Cece again.

She couldn't see her straight away so she approached the edge of the mezzanine, in case Cece had gone to a lower floor.

"Julienne," Cece said, from behind her.

Julienne turned to find her smiling at her.

"This is my favourite book," Cece said. "Have you read it?"

It was a collection of short stories by an author whose name Julienne didn't recognise.

"I haven't," she said.

"I'll buy it for you," Cece said, eyes lighting up. "I love short stories, little glimpses into another world."

"I like pretentious literary novels, mostly," Julienne said. "And romance."

Cece's eyes sparkled. "Who's your favorite author?"

"Zadie Smith."

"Interesting," Cece said, eyes narrowing. "I've read some of hers. I feel like I understand you much better now."

Julienne felt her cheeks heating up for probably the trillionth time that day. "Is that a good thing?"

Cece gave a sharp bark of a laugh. "It is! I love Zadie Smith."

"Do you just read short stories, or novels too?" Julienne asked.

"Oh, you know, I love a good thriller," Cece said. "Horror, too. And graphic novels! The characters become actors when they're drawn, instead of written."

"Don't they adapt a lot of TV shows from graphic novels? You should be in one," she said.

Cece snorted. "Yeah, and movies. I'd love to, but nobody's asked."

"One day," Julienne said.

"Maybe," Cece said, sounding a little uncertain. "I haven't even told Sadie it's something I'd like to do," she admitted.

"Why not?"

Cece bit her lip. "For a while we were so focused on proving I was a serious actress, y'know? Not just some wild former child star. So we picked projects pretty carefully."

"That sounds hard," Julienne said. "Always having to prove yourself."

Cece tilted her head to one side. "My mom had a plan for my career. Sadie has one too. It's what's best for longevity, or whatever."

"But what about what you actually want to do?"

"I already told you," Cece said, her tone sharp. "I don't know what I want."

"Sorry," Julienne said, quickly. It was clearly a sore point for Cece, that she didn't know what she wanted from her career. It seemed like a problem that was too big for Julienne to solve.

Cece shrugged. "It's okay," she said, and the tension dissolved. "Let's talk about something else."

"What's your favorite graphic novel?" Julienne asked, grateful for the reprieve.

Cece grinned. "I love The Wicked + The Divine. Have you heard of it?"

Julienne shook her head, and Cece explained what it was about. It sounded pretty cool, but Julienne wasn't really a graphic novel person.

"Hey," Cece said. "Why don't you pick me out a book? I picked one for you."

"Like what?"

"The whole point is that you choose," Cece said, but she was smiling as she said it.

Julienne bit her lip. More and more, this felt like a date. She wanted to pick out the perfect book for Cece, something that would impress her, but she felt ridiculous for even thinking about it.

She felt like she had something to prove.

"This is going to take you a while, isn't it?" Cece said. There was her knowing smirk again.

"There's a lot of books in here," Julienne said, praying she wasn't blushing.

Cece snorted. "I'll leave you to it."

It's just a book, Julienne told herself. It doesn't have to be anything more.

She thought of thrillers, and then dismissed that idea. All the thrillers she read were pure escapism. She didn't want to gift Cece just a few hours of escape. She tried not to think about all the meaning she was placing on this gift. It was just one book, just a single volume. It could be anything.

She strolled through the displays, looking for books she'd read recently and enjoyed. There was a brilliant satire, heavily promoted on the display, and a few prize winners that she'd read and liked. She paused in the LGBT+ book section, but she was scared of what that kind of book might insinuate.

She spent a few minutes in the biography section. She used to pore over the books of tennis stars when she was a teenager, kidding herself that she was going to be one. That Julienne felt like a different person now. None of those books stood out to her either, unless she wanted to give Cece a gift that said 'here's who I used to be'.

She was definitely overthinking it.

There was a whole section dedicated to the art galleries of LA, and she found herself thumbing through a coffee table book. It felt like home, it had most of her favorite local pieces, plus a few she hadn't seen. It was a book of everything she loved about LA. Her only worry was that it wouldn't be what Cece was expecting.

She met Cece at the cash register, feeling a little silly carrying her oversized hardback compared to Cece's stack of slim paperbacks. Cece had apparently decided to buy some more thrillers.

"I'm buying," Cece said, taking it out of Julienne's hands before she had a chance to protest.

"It's supposed to be a gift," she said anyway.

Cece shrugged and stepped up to the counter to pay.

"I wasn't expecting you to pick non-fiction," Cece said, as they took the lift back down to the parking lot.

"Don't worry, it's mostly pictures," Julienne said.

Cece grinned at her. "You're more fun when you're mean."

Julienne shrugged. "I don't know why you think I'm so boring."

"You were hired to be boring," Cece said. "You keep being more interesting than that."

Julienne tried to keep her smile contained as she climbed into Cece's car.

It had been a long time since anyone had been interested in Julienne.

FOURTEEN

By the time they'd got back to Cece's condo and eaten, they had to start getting ready to go out for the evening. Julienne felt a little more prepared for the party this time, since she'd at least met the host, but she still let Cece judge the three outfits she'd prepared.

Cece made her selection without much comment and then disappeared into her own room to get dressed.

Julienne put the dress on in the mirror and tried not to grimace at her reflection. It was an intensely purple dress with full-length gauzy sleeves that seemed to float around her arms. Reina had encouraged her to buy it, when they were browsing online, but she'd never had anywhere to wear it to.

Now was the time. She snapped a quick photo of herself and sent it to Reina with a dancing emoji as the caption, and then she settled on the floor to do her makeup.

She straightened her hair and combed down her bangs and applied silver eyeliner to each eyelid. She did the rest of her face, then finished with a dusky pink lipstick. She knocked on Cece's door to see if she was ready.

"You don't need to knock," Cece said.

Julienne pushed open the door. Whatever she planned to say to Cece caught in her throat as she took her in.

Cece was wearing a crisp white shirt that was open over her cleavage and a carefully structured velvet blazer that might as well have been a cape. Beneath it, she wore black jeans that clung to her thighs and stiletto heels.

"Good, right?" Cece said. She was smirking.

It took a second for Julienne to find words. "I feel underdressed," she said, looking down at herself.

"You look amazing, babe," Cece said. She grabbed a clutch bag from where it was hanging on a doorknob.

Julienne mumbled a quiet "thanks" and followed Cece downstairs, her heels echoing in the quiet house.

"We can walk to Joshua's," Cece said, shutting the door behind her. "His place is like two blocks away."

"Don't your feet hurt?" Julienne asked. She'd never got used to wearing heels, and avoided it as much as possible.

Cece shrugged. "Practice," she said.

It didn't take long for them to arrive at Joshua's. His house looked a lot like Cece's, except the outside walls were a little paler and dark bricks marked the path. There were more plants, too, some Julienne recognised as local.

Cece just opened the door and strolled right in, not bothering to knock or announce her presence. Julienne followed her in, but she was getting a little tired of always trailing in Cece's wake.

Cece gave Joshua an enthusiastic hug and handed him a bag Julienne hadn't noticed her carrying.

"Oh Cee, you shouldn't have," Joshua said, grinning.

"Don't even," Cece said. "As if you'd let me forget."

Joshua glanced at Julienne, confusion on his face for a

moment before he recognised her. "You're still here? I'm impressed."

"She's not that bad, it turns out," Cece said.

Joshua laughed. "That means she really likes you," he said.

Julienne flushed. "Happy birthday," she said.

"Thank you, I love your dress," Joshua said. "Go enjoy the party, loves. It's gonna be a good one."

He winked at Julienne. Cece caught her by the wrist and tugged her away, into the kitchen. There were a few people in there already, but the house wasn't nearly as crowded as the last party. Not yet, at least.

"Do you want a drink?" Cece asked.

"Sure," Julienne said, without thinking about it.

Cece raised her eyebrows and filled two plastic cups from a large jug of something brightly coloured.

"Joshua gets the best cocktails," Cece said.

"How old is he?" Julienne asked, suddenly realizing she might be the only person at this party legally allowed to drink.

"He's twenty," Cece said. "Don't worry about it, babe."

Julienne felt like the frequency of Cece calling her babe was increasing, and she didn't know how to feel about it. She took a long swig of her drink instead, deciding that that was easier than trying to guess what Cece was thinking.

She couldn't taste the alcohol at all, which almost always meant drinking it was a bad idea.

Cece watched her, grinning. "Take it slow," she said.

Julienne remembered she was supposed to be working, but it felt like it was too late now. And she wasn't sure she could watch Cece get drunk and stay sober, not with the week they'd had. Not with all the moments Cece had been close enough to embrace.

"I want to show you Joshua's place, it's awesome," Cece said. She refilled both of their cups to the brim and they left the kitchen via the patio door.

"I smoked my first joint in his garage," Cece said, pointing. "His mom was so mad when she found us."

"This is her place?" Julienne asked, looking around.

"Not anymore," Cece said. "She visits a lot, though."

A tall, skinny girl seemed to recognise Cece and reached out for a hug.

"Allie!" Cece said. "I didn't know you were coming."

"Please," Allie said, taking a drag on a cigarette. She was the only person who seemed to be smoking instead of vaping. "I wouldn't miss it, babes."

Julienne took a swig of her drink.

"This is my friend Jules," Cece said. "Me and Allie used to work together."

Julienne smiled and nodded. She watched something be silently communicated between the two of them, but she had no idea what it was.

There was a brief conversation about the music, and what Allie had got Joshua for his birthday, and then Julienne realised her cup was empty and so was Cece's.

"I'm gonna get you another drink," Cece said. "You good?"

Julienne blinked. Her head felt warm. "Sure," she said.

"So are you guys, like, dating or what?" Allie asked, as soon as Cece was out of earshot.

"No," Julienne said. She didn't know what else to say. "Just friends."

Allie hummed. "I've met all of Cece's friends. You're new."

Julienne shrugged. "Sadie introduced us," she said.

Allie raised one eyebrow and Julienne felt small

beneath her gaze. "Okay," she said, but it was laced with suspicion. Julienne wondered if all Cece's friends were protective; if that was what she inspired in people.

"So you're an actress?" Julienne asked, trying to make conversation.

"Not anymore," Allie said. "I'm doing music, now. More chance to travel."

"What kind of music?"

Allie gave her a disdainful look. "Pop," she said. She took another drag of her cigarette and exhaled. The smoke blew in Julienne's face.

Cece returned mercifully quickly.

"I brought you a present," she said. She held out her hand, in it another cup of cocktail and a shot glass held carefully between two fingers. "Tequila."

Julienne groaned.

Cece grinned at her. "Everyone likes tequila."

"I like it a bit too much," Julienne said. "No lime?"

"I only had two hands, gimme a break."

Julienne took the two drinks from Cece. They knocked their shot glasses against each other with a soft plastic clunk and tossed them back.

Julienne winced. She hated it without the lime to chase. She took a swig of the cocktail.

"Hey," Cece said. "Do you want to dance?"

It took a moment for Julienne to register the hand stretched out for her to take. She blinked and shook her head. She took Cece's hand, surprised by how off-balance she felt when standing.

The tequila was maybe a mistake. She just wanted to relax a little. She hadn't wanted to lose control.

The three of them walked side by side back into the house, and Julienne shivered as the bass thump grew louder.

The volume had been turned way up since she was last inside. Her heartbeat thudded as she followed Cece and Allie into a dark, crowded room. The lighting strobed. Sweat began to bead at her temples.

The three of them danced together a little, and then Joshua appeared out of the dark and took Cece's hand. He spun her around and Julienne found herself laughing and laughing and one song blurred into the next as they kept dancing. The four of them were interconnected, hands brushing against each other, sometimes shoulders, sometimes hips. Julienne fell and Cece picked up her, her hands a sticky comfort, and then she was upright and moving and dancing. She could feel the grin plastered on her face, the sweat-stickiness of her hair. The crowd moved too, shunting them one way or another, but her and Cece stayed connected all the same.

Joshua seemed to disappear as fast as he'd arrived, and then Allie was gone too, and it was just her and Cece, dancing together. They moved together, their limbs not quite in sync, and Julienne felt every brush of Cece's body against hers.

Julienne tried to remember this was work, that she should be staying in control, but her limbs were too loose and the music too loud and it felt like none of it mattered any more.

She didn't know when they'd gotten so close, when she'd stopped being able to tell if the body heat was hers or Cece's.

The music went quiet for a moment and their bodies stilled and Julienne found her eyes catching on the shape of Cece's lips, plump and dark with lipstick. She wondered what it would be like to kiss them, to take a chance and press her lips against Cece's. She wondered if Cece would let her.

Cece leaned in close, really close, and Julienne's throat went dry, the possibility of it unbearable. "Do you want to get some air?" Cece yelled in her ear.

Julienne nodded mutely.

She couldn't tell if she was relieved or disappointed.

FIFTEEN

Cece led the way out of the dancefloor, and soon it felt like the air was growing colder and the crowd thinner.

She was sure she looked a mess, sweaty and happy and drunk. She was about to ask Cece her opinion, but she found Cece already watching her, a curious expression on her face.

Something knotted in her gut.

"Let's get you some water," Cece said, and led her back to the kitchen.

It wasn't until Cece let go to turn on the faucet that Julienne realised they'd been holding hands the entire time.

"Drink up," Cece said, passing her the glass.

Julienne followed orders. Cece watched as she drank.

"You're really quiet," Cece said, her voice softer than Julienne had ever heard of it.

Julienne bit her lip. "I didn't mean to get this drunk," she said.

"I don't think most drunk people do."

Julienne refilled her glass and carried on drinking, waiting for Cece to say something else. The kitchen was almost eerily quiet, save for the bass thumping from the other room. It felt peaceful, an oasis of calm.

"You're so independent," Cece said, conversationally. "You don't seem to need anyone."

"What?"

"Nothing," Cece said.

The silence stretched between them. Julienne didn't dare look at Cece. She felt the world might tilt on its axis if she did.

"I'm gonna go say hi to some people," Cece said. "Are you okay to stay here?"

Julienne nodded. She felt like a child, as if she were the underage drinker who'd had too much. She hated that their roles seemed to have reversed. She wondered if she should feel hurt that Cece was leaving for someone she found more interesting.

"Hey," Cece said. "I had a really good day today."

A strange expression appeared on her face, and for a moment, Julienne wondered if Cece was going to cry. It passed in an instant, and a sharp grin replaced it, and all of Cece's vibrancy returned.

The door to the kitchen swung shut behind Cece and Julienne was left alone.

She thought about raiding the freezer in search of ice cream, or better yet some fries, but she wasn't sure if Joshua would be okay with that, and Julienne still wanted him to like her. It seemed like his opinion mattered to Cece. She sat on the counter, drumming her fingers against it in time to the beat, and wondered how long she was supposed to wait here.

Her head felt heavy and tired. People came into the kitchen and left without speaking to her and she wondered if she was completely invisible in this house full of people who were larger than life.

The minutes dragged by. She tugged out her phone and sent Tori a silly selfie, typed out a message to Reina and then deleted it. She hadn't told Reina anything about the job, and she wasn't sure she trusted herself to keep to the NDA in this state.

She washed her glass up in the sink and left it face down on the counter, just for something to do. Her stupid dress was damp with sweat and a little rumpled, and she caught sight of her face in the window reflection. Shiny and smudged and a little wild-eyed.

She wanted to go home.

Something about being drunk and alone in this place made her feel very small, and she decided it was time to look for Cece. She walked back through the house, around the edge of the room with the music, into another dimly lit room, one sofa occupied by a couple having a conversation in low voices.

She got lost, briefly, somehow circling back to the kitchen, and she felt a lump form in her throat as she realised how screwed she was if she couldn't find Cece. She was still drunk, and she held on to the handrail like a life preserver as she climbed the stairs to look for Cece.

An irrational thought in the back of her brain said 'she's left without you', but she tried not to give it any attention.

It was quieter upstairs, aside from a few people loitering outside the restroom. Julienne hoped she'd find Cece soon, because she wasn't sure she could find her way back to the kitchen on her own. She could hear voices at the end of the corridor, and she followed the sound to a door that was slightly open, a wedge of light spilling out into the corridor.

She hesitated. She wasn't sure if she should knock. But then she heard Cece's bright, certain laugh.

Finally! She pushed open the door. Three people, Cece and Allie and someone she didn't recognise, sat on the floor around a coffee table.

It took a moment to register the metal straw in Cece's hand, the mirror, the lines of white powder.

Cece looked up as the door opened and smiled, her grin a little manic, eyes too wide.

"Who the fuck are you?" said the one Julienne didn't know.

Cece blinked, registering. "Shit," she said. "Julienne!" She leapt up, knocking the coffee table with a thunk.

"You know her?"

Cece waved a hand dismissively at them. "Hi Jules," she said, words coming out of her mouth at spitfire speed. "I totally lost track of time! Are you feeling better?"

"Are you out of your mind?" Julienne asked. Her voice didn't sound like her own, pitchy and louder than usual, and Julienne felt very far away from the coffee table, the powder, the party.

"I'm good, it's all good," Cece said. "We're just having a good night, aren't we?"

Allie made a noise of confirmation, then muttered something to the other person, who was already leaning over the table, snorting up the powder.

Cece was a little too close to Julienne, bouncing on her heels, eyes wide. "You feeling better?" Cece asked, for the second time. "Let's talk in the corridor, okay?"

That was what she'd come up here to tell Cece, she remembered. She wanted to go home. She was a little shell-shocked, a little drunk, standing in front of Cece, white powder still on her nose, trying to act like this was normal.

"I want to go home," Julienne said. It felt like the only thing she could really articulate right now. "What's going on?"

Cece tried to shepherd Julienne towards the door but Julienne was rooted, unmoving.

"It's just coke," Cece tried. "It's nothing, not a big deal. Don't you want to talk about this in private?"

Julienne couldn't take her eyes off Cece. Cece ran a hand through her hair, looking like her nerves were not just frayed but jagged at the edges. She glanced back at her friends and shifted uneasily from foot to foot, and Julienne wondered what she was supposed to *do*.

"You're high," Julienne said. Her words came to her slowly, and nausea rolled in her stomach. "Should I call Sadie?"

They weren't really having a conversation, just saying things at each other. Her phone was already in her hand.

Cece stepped closer, entering Julienne's personal space. With her heels on, they were the same height, and it was much more imposing than Julienne was used to from Cece.

"Don't do that," Cece said, her voice terse.

"It's my job," Julienne said. Her words felt thick, like they were dragged out of her throat.

"Yeah, and you're drunk," Cece spat. Julienne flinched. "Who do you think she's gonna be more mad at? Me or you?"

Julienne felt her eyes beginning to well up. "I'm sorry, okay!" she said, louder than she meant to. "I just want to go home. Please?"

Cece shook her head, frustrated. "It's so early, Julienne," she said. "We were just getting started, for fuck's sake."

"You have work in the morning," Julienne said. She

hated that she sounded like she was begging. "Let's just call it a night."

Cece glanced back at the table, at the other two. She sighed, irritation written on her face. "I should just call you an Uber," she said, "and carry on with my life."

Julienne was shaking her head before Cece had finished speaking. "I'm not leaving you." Even drunk, she was still certain that was the right decision. "I'll be glued to your side if you stay, even if I'm drunk. No more coke."

Cece met her eyes again. "Fine," she conceded. "We'll go home. One condition: you don't call Sadie."

For some reason, Julienne felt like she needed to apologise. She looked into Cece's eyes, her pupils like a vast black hole, and tried to remember why she was here.

"Wait," said Not-Allie, "are you guys like, a couple?"

"Shut up, B," Cece said.

That was it, wasn't it? They weren't a couple. They weren't anything. They weren't even friends. Just because she'd enjoyed spending time with Cece, just because Cece had been kind to her, didn't mean Julienne could trust her.

"Were you going to come back and get me?" Julienne asked, keeping her voice low. She felt achingly vulnerable. Cece had left her, drunk and alone in a house full of strangers. She wasn't even sure she had any right to be upset. Cece was right – she shouldn't have gotten drunk.

Cece nodded. "I just, I got sidetracked. It's a party. I was going to come back." Her words still came too quick, spilling out her mouth.

Julienne bit her lip.

"It's not a big deal," Cece said. "I was coming right back."

Cece's face was still a little too close, taking up all of Julienne's vision, and she took a step back. She needed to put more distance between them, suddenly. She needed space.

"Can we go now?" Julienne asked.

Cece got out her phone and showed Julienne she was ordering an Uber. "They won't miss me. Let's go wait outside, okay?"

Julienne allowed herself to be steered out of the room, Cece's hand hot on her upper arm. Cece took a brief detour to say goodbye to Joshua and wished him happy birthday again, and by then they were holding hands and Julienne wasn't sure how that happened. Joshua made a comment about them leaving early but Cece shot Joshua a look she couldn't read and Julienne gave up on trying to figure out any of it.

The front of the house was quiet. They stood apart from the trio of strangers also waiting for rides by the curb, having a too-loud conversation in the LA night.

Julienne didn't say anything. They were still holding hands. Cece was silent, too, but fidgeting constantly, rocking on her heels. Julienne watched as she took out the vape pen and sucked greedily on it.

She shouldn't have trusted Cece. She shouldn't have gotten drunk; she shouldn't have taken that drink. She was so involved in the life of this girl she barely knew.

She was wrung out, exhausted.

They didn't exchange a word the whole journey home, nor as Cece unlocked the door and they made their way upstairs.

"Jules," Cece said, standing at the doorway to her bedroom. She looked like she was searching for the right words. "This doesn't have to be a big deal."

Julienne stared at her. "Cece..." she trailed off. She didn't know what to say.

Cece shrugged, gave her a small smile.

"Goodnight," Cece said, and walked away.

Julienne stared at her closed bedroom door for longer than she'd like to admit.

She didn't know how to come back from this.

SIXTEEN

Julienne was awake in bed for an hour before her alarm went off. Her mouth tasted like bile but she couldn't summon the motivation to get out of bed and face the day.

She didn't want to wake Cece for work. She didn't know what to say to her, what she was supposed to do. She wished she hadn't drunk so much.

It felt worse than the Adderall. They knew each other better, now, she'd spent days in Cece's space, in her *life*. She didn't know how to pair the Cece that had made sure Julienne was drinking water when she was drunk, with the Cece that did coke at parties and abandoned her. Maybe it was just the alcohol that made that so jarring – maybe it was something else.

She got up and brushed her teeth eventually, and then knocked lightly on Cece's door before walking in. Cece's bare leg poked out from under the white covers, and Cece looked blearily at her. The room was tidier than they'd left it yesterday, and Julienne wondered if Cece had stayed up late tidying it.

"Yeah?" Cece said, voice groggy from sleep.

"I'm going to go to the gym," she said. "You need to be on set in three hours."

Cece pushed herself upright, holding onto the sheets to keep herself covered. She looked rumpled, vulnerable. "Are you coming back?" Cece asked.

Julienne wondered if it meant something that the only time Cece cared about modesty was when she thought Julienne was mad at her.

Julienne swallowed. She should be mad at her, but she couldn't quite conjure up anger when Cece looked so small. "Do you want me to?" she asked, instead.

Cece looked away. "Only if you want to be here," she mumbled.

Julienne sighed. "Do you want me to come with you to set?"

"Maybe? I don't know."

Julienne had never seen Cece look so small.

"I'll be back in two hours," Julienne said.

Cece just nodded.

There were so many things Julienne wanted to say, but she didn't say any of them. She just left.

She needed time to clear her head.

She went to the gym first, putting her headphones in and not speaking to anyone for a solid hour. She barely even thought, just concentrated on the strain in her muscles. She pushed herself harder than she usually did, and went straight home after. She needed to stand in her own shower and let the water wash off the gym sweat and that morning-after staleness.

She made a quick breakfast, knowing Cece's unreliable approach to food, and then she ran out of excuses not to go back. She needed to make sure Cece got to work on time. She should probably make sure Cece ate something, too.

She let herself in the front door of Cece's condo and called out for her, and Cece appeared out of the kitchen wearing just an oversized t-shirt. She yawned and stretched, lifting the shirt to show more of her thighs. She seemed back to her usual self.

"I'll be ready to go in half an hour," Cece said. "Can you drive?"

Julienne nodded.

She didn't follow Cece upstairs. The living room was still a mess from all the painting, and Julienne fought the urge to pace. She peeled up the painter's tape around the edges and threw it in the bin. It gave her something to do with her hands; it made her feel less like she was failing Cece.

She turned on the TV and flicked absent-mindedly through the channels, perching on the edge of the couch. The minutes seem to stretch out. She didn't know what to do with herself.

She flicked the TV off when she heard Cece coming down the stairs, trying to steel herself for whatever the day would bring.

"Let's go," Cece said, tone carefree.

Julienne wondered if it was all an act. "Are you gonna eat something?"

"I'll get something on set," Cece said breezily.

She hummed softly under her breath as she followed Julienne to the car. Julienne couldn't understand her mood. Once they were in the car, Cece started hitting buttons on the radio, trying to find a channel or connect her phone.

Julienne turned it off with a slap of her hand once she was on the road. "I don't know the way, I need to concentrate."

Cece sat back in her seat. "Okay."

Julienne hesitated. "We should talk about last night."

"My mom used to do this," Cece said. Julienne could hear the smirk in her voice. "Make me have difficult conversations in the car so we wouldn't have to make eye contact."

Julienne sighed. "What do you want me to say?"

"I don't have a drug problem," Cece said.

Julienne concentrated on the road to keep from rolling her eyes.

"You've never been invited to a party and wanted to try it?"

"No."

"Okay," Cece said. "What about ecstasy or poppers or weed? It's just fun at parties."

"Cocaine is one of the most addictive drugs," Julienne said. She'd done some googling on her phone in bed that morning.

"Name five of your favorite actresses. I bet they all do it," Cece said.

Julienne didn't say anything as she left the freeway. She didn't want to set off Cece's temper, but something about Cece's blasé approach rubbed her the wrong way.

"What about your career?"

"I'm here, aren't I?" Cece said. Julienne pulled into the parking lot of the studio. When the car was motionless, she turned and met Cece's eyes.

"How late would you have stayed out partying if it weren't for me?" Julienne asked. "Would you have bothered getting up this morning?"

Cece rolled her eyes.

Julienne ran a hand through her hair. "Looking out for you is literally my job. I screwed up last night, I know. I shouldn't have gotten drunk." She hesitated for a moment, and then spat out the words before she could change her mind: "I trusted you, Cece."

"You knew what you signed up for," Cece said, not meeting Julienne's eyes. "If you don't like it, you can go."

Before Julienne could come up with a response, Cece had flung the car door open and launched herself out, stalking across the parking lot.

Julienne took a few deep breaths before she got out of the car and followed. She hoped she didn't owe anyone an apology for Cece's mood.

When she entered the studio, though, the atmosphere was entirely different. Cece was talking to one of her costars, a script in her hand, and there was even a smile on her face. Sam passed by and gave Julienne a smile and a nod, and Julienne just blinked at the scene in front of her.

She headed over to Cece. Her smile stayed in place as Julienne approached, but Julienne felt a shiver run down her spine as their eyes met.

"Shall I just hang out in your trailer until you're done?" Julienne asked.

Cece gave a one-shouldered shrug. "Whatever," she said. "I can get a ride home from someone else."

"She's been around a bit," one of Cece's colleagues said as Julienne was walking away. "You dating?"

Cece sputtered a laugh and Julienne felt the heat of shame on her cheeks. God, what was she doing here? Trying to act like Cece's friend was literally in her job description, and yet Cece kept pushing her away.

She didn't want to be around Cece.

She gave herself the rest of the day off, and probably drove too fast to get home. She was angry, but she wasn't even sure if it was at Cece or herself. If Cece got caught doing coke, they'd probably both lose their jobs. If Cece fucked up at work because of the coke, they'd definitely both lose their jobs.

Julienne wasn't ready for that.

And the worst part of it was that she'd really believed Cece was going to do better.

Tori was out, which was just as well, because Julienne didn't know if she could talk about last night without breaking her NDA. She found a documentary on Netflix instead, and settled in to get completely distracted for a few hours. It helped to focus on big, untouchable problems, things she couldn't solve or prevent, like climate change or the opioid crisis.

She fell asleep on the couch before the end of the documentary, only waking up when Tori let herself in the apartment door.

Her phone flashed at her. A missed call from Cece.

Pretty much the last person she wanted to hear from when she was still groggy from her nap.

She waved at Tori and went into her room to call Cece back, hoping her voice wasn't as awful as she felt.

"Hey," Cece said, picking up on the first ring.

Julienne cleared her throat. "What's up?" she asked.

Nothing, for a second. Then: "I'm sorry," Cece said. "I shouldn't have ditched you."

Julienne bit her lip. It wasn't the whole problem, but it was a start.

"Do you want to come to Vegas on Monday?" Cece said.

Julienne was glad Cece couldn't see the face she was pulling. "To party?" Julienne clarified.

Cece laughed. "No, it's a photoshoot. Sadie doesn't want me to go on my own, and I thought it could be fun. It's just a day trip."

Julienne thought about it for a moment. "I'll come but... I do want to talk about the coke. Seriously."

Cece's sigh crackled through the phone. "Okay," she said. "Just not right now. Okay?"

"Soon," Julienne said. "But it's a deal."

"I'll get Sadie to book you a ticket," Cece said, and Julienne could hear the smile in her voice. "It'll be fun! The flight is at 7am, I'll pick you up at 5.30?"

"You don't need me to wake you?" Julienne asked.

"Nah, it's all good. I'm gonna get an early night. See you tomorrow, okay?"

Julienne said her goodbyes and hung up. She let out a long, ragged sigh.

She liked Cece way more than she should. Cece's mood was so unpredictable; Julienne wasn't sure this bout of contrition would last.

Somehow she still found herself looking forward to seeing Cece again.

SEVENTEEN

It had only been a week, but it already felt like her whole world revolved around Cece. She had messages from her parents and friends she hadn't replied to, and she'd barely spoken to Tori all week.

It was exhausting.

Cece called her just when she was starting to worry about getting to the airport in time, and she headed downstairs. Cece hadn't told her to bring anything, so she just brought her handbag and a book to read, imagining there would be downtime during the photoshoot.

When she got in Cece's car, she was gratified to see that Cece looked as tired as Julienne felt. The sun was just peeking over the horizon.

"Ready?" Cece asked.

Julienne nodded.

The short drive to the airport passed in silence, and then the two of them were walking in step across the parking lot.

"I should warn you," Cece said. "I'm just going straight to sleep when we get on that plane."

Julienne shrugged. "Is anyone else coming?"

Cece shook her head. "We'll meet everyone there."

Cece scanned their tickets in the machine and then they had to queue for security. Julienne didn't realise where Cece was leading her at first, until they were in the priority lane for first class tickets. She didn't know how much money Cece had, but she seemed to be unfailingly generous.

In her head, Julienne totted up the plane tickets, the books, the offer for her to buy anything she wanted at the store, plus who knew what else would come up today.

Julienne wasn't sure if it was because money didn't matter to Cece or she just didn't know how to budget. It just seemed like their scale of acceptable spending was vastly different.

They were welcomed into the premium lounge with a smile after they'd made it through security, and someone came around to offer them drinks after they had settled into the leather seats.

"I've never flown anything other than economy," Julienne admitted, picking up a magazine from the selection arranged on the table.

"Did you visit home much when you were in college?"

Julienne shook her head. "Not really. I stayed most summers for internships."

Cece hummed. "You like LA that much?"

"Yeah," Julienne said. "I always wanted to come back to California after we moved to England. I had so many good memories here, and then I got into UCLA and the rest is history."

"California's not all that," Cece said.

"You don't like it?"

"I've been here since I was ten, but it never really felt like home. It's where the work is, it's where my friends are."

The gate announcement interrupted their conversation, so Julienne didn't get the chance to ask where Cece would really like to live. They joined the short line for premium boarding, sandwiched between two tall men in business suits.

Julienne felt underdressed.

"I love flying," Cece confided in Julienne. "I wish I had an excuse to travel more."

Their first class seats weren't much more impressive than the coach ones Julienne was familiar with, just a little extra room to recline and a nicer seat.

Cece flashed her a grin as they sat down, and then put her earbuds in. Julienne was kind of impressed to see that Cece really did fall asleep straight after take off.

She took a deep breath, trying to relax. For a little while, Julienne had been able to forget about what a disaster the last few days had been. Cece had that power somehow, to make everything seem so normal. It was like the tension between them had evaporated.

It was something she couldn't help but admire about Cece. It was hard to feel awkward around her, because she was so willing to let Julienne in. It was like her superpower.

She flicked through the magazine, telling herself not to overthink anything about Cece. It was more a way to pass the time than something she was actually interested in, but she wanted to save her book for later.

By the time she'd finished reading, the seatbelt sign was back on and they were preparing for landing. Cece woke up groggily as people began to stand up and take their bags from the overhead lockers, and they disembarked together.

"What do you want for breakfast?" Cece said.

Julienne looked around the airport, a little overwhelmed by the choice.

Cece laughed. "Don't worry, we're not eating here."

There was a driver holding a sign with Cece's name on it waiting by the exit, and they climbed in the back of a shiny black car with dark tinted windows. The seats were plush leather, and Cece said something to the driver that Julienne didn't catch.

"I'm gonna call ahead, get some food waiting for us when we get there," Cece said.

Julienne was starting to wonder if this whole trip was some kind of bribe. She was falling for it, a little bit, drawn in by Cece's enthusiasm and the way she seemed, for once, to be coolly in control of everything.

"Have you been to Vegas before?" Julienne asked.

Cece shook her head. "I'm not old enough to do anything fun here. Maybe for my 21st birthday, but that's in a few years."

"I came for a friend's 21st but we were all in college and barely had a budget," Julienne said. "I don't remember much of the weekend, to be honest."

Cece laughed, delighted. "My kind of weekend."

Julienne regretted telling her that already.

"I figure Vegas is a lot like Times Square," Cece said. "All the pretty lights all over the place, everything super expensive."

"I've never been to New York," Julienne said.

"I'll have to take you there someday," Cece said, oh so casual, and Julienne felt something flutter in her chest.

Their journey took an hour or so, and when Julienne got out of the car she realised why they'd got on a plane to shoot on the dry lakes of the Nevada desert. She hadn't ventured outside the strip last time she'd been here, too focused on celebrating, but the lake beds were worth a trip.

Cece didn't appear to notice the beauty of their

surroundings, just walking straight over to a group of people crowded outside the entrance of the trailer. One of them greeted her with an enthusiastic hug.

It took Julienne a moment to follow her over, still a little distracted by the vast empty space they found themselves in. The lake beds seemed to stretch on as far as the eye could see.

Cece directed her to a little table set up outside the trailer. Conversation drifted around them, Cece occasionally chiming in with an opinion on the styling, but Julienne was too focused on the array of pastries on the table to really pay attention. Cece still managed to finish eating before her and disappeared into the trailer. Julienne swallowed the last few mouthfuls of pain au chocolat and followed her in.

The trailer was cramped and too warm, and Julienne sat beside Cece, listening to the discussion with the makeup artist.

"Can you take pictures on this?" Cece asked, thrusting her phone at Julienne. "And put it on charge when you're done."

Julienne frowned. She wasn't Cece's assistant and she didn't particularly like being ordered around.

"Sorry," Cece said. "It's like, 10 minutes of your time, and then you can chill and enjoy the view, I promise."

"Alright," Julienne said. She hadn't realised Cece had noticed how much she liked the location.

The makeup artist pulled a silly pose behind Cece and Julienne snapped a few photos. She waited till Cece was a bit more made up and took a few more, then plugged it in to charge. She pulled out the book she'd brought to read and settled in on the chair beside Cece, trying to concentrate on it.

"You didn't bring the book I gave you?" Cece asked.

Julienne blinked. "I think I left it at yours, actually."

"Oh," Cece said. "I want to know what you think, when you read it."

"Okay," Julienne said. "You too, with the art book."

Cece grinned at her. "I already started, there was this one piece I really liked-" She was starting to get animated, and the makeup artist silenced her with a tap to the forehead.

"We'll talk about it another time," Cece said quietly, trying not to move her face.

It was funny how unnatural it seemed, Cece not being her full expressive self.

It was so easy to talk to Cece, forget about the party and the theatrics of it all. That was the thing, she was always so easy to talk to, it almost made Julienne forget there was something more going on.

Julienne tried to refocus on her book. Cece was scrolling through her phone as the makeup artist dabbed at her face. Outside, Julienne could see people moving around the camera and the reflectors. The constant movement was distracting.

"Hey," Cece said. "You don't even follow me on Instagram."

Julienne looked up from the book she wasn't really reading anyway. "I don't?"

"You don't," Cece said, keeping her face still but using her phone to gesture at Julienne. "I tagged you in that photo."

"I don't really use social media that much," Julienne said. She placed her bookmark in the book and closed it, getting her phone out. "I can do it now."

Cece made a noise like she was satisfied. "You should follow Joshua, too."

"All my notifications are from you," Julienne said, furrowing her brow as she looked down at her phone. "That photo."

"We looked hot," Cece said, sounding smug about it.

She hit the follow button on Cece's profile, the verified blue tick seeming to wink at her. She scrolled through her profile and couldn't help but notice Cece's familiar smirk and the way she courted her followers' attention.

Had Cece already seen the way she held Julienne's attention? That smirk seemed so knowing, now. A thrill of fear ran through Julienne, and for the first time, she wondered if Cece was just using her, if Cece found her easy to manipulate so she could say she was trying to be better.

Julienne kept trying to make all the chaos of Cece's life into order, but so far Cece hadn't changed her behavior at all.

For all she knew, Cece wasn't trying at all.

EIGHTEEN

"We're heading outside for the shoot," Cece said, tapping on her shoulder. "Come watch."

She didn't wait for a response from Julienne before she left the trailer. Julienne left her bag by the makeup table and followed the entourage outside.

It wasn't until they were out in the sun that Julienne really took in Cece's outfit. She was wearing a dress made of something soft and translucent, a woven black material that floated over her body. Beneath it she wore fifties style lingerie, in a cream floral pattern that was bright against her light brown skin.

As Cece moved in the sun, Julienne noticed the thin gold jewellery that caressed her waist, and her mouth went dry.

Cece's smile was as bright as ever as she moved over to where the photographer was setting up, making playful conversation with the stylist and someone from the magazine.

Julienne realised she was staring. Everyone else was

watching Cece, too, but she supposed it was their job to do so. Julienne was just captivated.

The photographer indicated she was ready and Julienne watched as Cece transformed in front of her eyes, just as she did on set. Instead of her usual energetic self, Cece became demure and elegant. Her body moved smoothly from one pose to the next, using the landscape to her benefit.

The desert heat meant the makeup artist was called in for touch ups quickly, and then a few more poses and an outfit change. Cece disappeared back inside briefly. Julienne watched the photographer and her assistant change the angles of the camera and get out some props while Cece changed. When she returned, Cece was dressed in a way that showed her youth far more. In the last ensemble, Julienne had almost forgotten Cece was only nineteen – she played a high schooler on a TV show, for crying out loud – but now her age was clear. She was wearing a shift dress made from delicate white lace, with carefully chosen accessories: an intricate silver bracelet around her ankle and a flower pinned into her hair, coral pink against the golden blonde.

Cece began to pose against an arch the team had set up. The morning light and something the makeup artist had done made her skin seem to glow. Cece toyed with the effect, playing with the scattered shadows cast by the interlocking bars of the archway, letting it add dimension to her hair, her skin, her dress.

An assistant moved in and adjusted something, another quick makeup break, an instruction Julienne didn't catch.

She moved a little closer to the scene to watch, mesmerised. Cece stretched upwards, the tip of her fingers curling around a bar of the arch, and their eyes met.

The white of the dress brought out the rich brown of her eyes, and Julienne felt it like a punch to the stomach. The camera clicked, but Cece didn't move, staying completely still as they locked eyes.

The moment lingered. It felt as though the whole world had slowed down.

Someone spoke and Cece broke her gaze, shifting into another pose. Julienne shivered, in spite of the heat.

Her phone buzzed and snapped her out of the strange trance she was in. Sadie had texted her, wanting to catch up and talk about how her first week had been.

Julienne couldn't believe it was only a week. It felt like a lifetime.

She didn't know what to say to Sadie. There was so much to explain – Sam, the coke, the days they'd spent painting – that she didn't even know where to start. She didn't know how to explain the coke without admitting that she'd been drunk on the job, either.

Not to mention the feelings for Cece she was struggling to compartmentalise.

The photoshoot was over before she got totally lost in her thoughts and a car arrived to take them back to Las Vegas.

"So that's it? We're done?" Julienne asked. She was a little surprised they'd flown for only a few hours.

"Not yet," Cece said. "There's an interview, too. I'm meeting the writer at Planet Hollywood."

"Do you want me to come?" Julienne asked.

Cece shook her head. "I'll call you when I'm done."

"Okay," Julienne said, feeling a little unsure. She didn't really know what to do in Las Vegas all by herself. She didn't want to drink or gamble on her own.

"Go have some fun," Cece said. "We're both getting paid for this, remember."

"I don't really gamble."

Cece laughed. "Do you take any risks?"

"Hanging out with you," Julienne shot back, trying to ignore the twist in her stomach at Cece's words.

"I guess I deserved that," Cece said.

Julienne didn't meet her eyes as she settled back in her seat, and the rest of the journey passed in silence. Eventually, the car deposited them outside Planet Hollywood, and Cece disappeared inside with barely a flick of her wrist in goodbye.

Julienne looked up and down the Vegas strip at a bit of a loss for what to do. She ended up wandering around the malls, looking at things she couldn't afford and wasn't sure she wanted anyway. It was a futile way to pass an hour and it made her feel frustrated and irritable.

She couldn't get Cece out of her head.

Searching for a distraction, she wandered into the Planet Hollywood casino. It was a strange place during the day time, and she was reluctant to put any money on the table. She remembered the last time she'd been here, her and Reina daring each other to bet increasing amounts. Reina had won some money. Julienne had lost a little.

She was too cautious, Reina had said then. Julienne wondered if that was still true.

It made her a little sad to walk through the casino all by herself, remembering when she'd been celebrating a birthday surrounded by her friends. She turned down more than one free drink in the half hour she spent in there.

She was deciding what to do next when her phone rang, and she answered on her way out the door, grateful for a reprieve.

"Hey, I'm all done," Cece said. "Meet me where the car dropped us off?"

Julienne agreed and hung up the phone, crossing the mall plaza quickly to get outside.

Cece was already waiting for her in the dry desert heat, looking perfectly relaxed.

"Good interview?" she asked.

Cece shrugged. "Hopefully. It's a bit of a flashier magazine than I'm used to. Sadie wants me out there as a serious up-and-comer, not just another child star. She thinks casting directors will notice."

"The photoshoot was good," Julienne said.

Cece smiled at her. "It was, wasn't it?"

Julienne held her gaze for a moment too long. She looked elsewhere, but didn't know what she was supposed to be looking for. She didn't even know how much time they had before the flight.

"So," Cece said. "I owe you an apology."

Julienne swallowed.

"I booked us a table at this Italian place," Cece said. "I looked up some reviews."

Once again, Julienne found herself wondering if she was being bribed. Maybe this was just how Cece apologised.

They walked down the strip, following directions on Cece's phone. Cece kept stopping to take in the bright lights.

"How does it compare to Times Square?" Julienne asked.

"I like it more, I think," Cece said. "There's no fountains in Times Square."

Julienne laughed. "Does Times Square have an Eiffel Tower?"

Cece grinned at her. "Does imitation Paris offend you?"

"It's not as good as the real thing. We spent two weeks there just before I came here for college."

"It's so easy to travel in Europe, I'm jealous," Cece said. "I bet you've seen tons of it."

"We used to go skiing in Italy," Julienne offered, feeling a little sheepish. "I went on a school trip once."

"I've never been skiing," Cece said.

"I love it," Julienne said. "I haven't been in years, though."

"You can ski in America," Cece pointed out.

Julienne shrugged. "I guess I just never got around to it."

The conversation drifted, and Julienne forgot that she'd ever been mad at Cece. She made that so easy, somehow.

They arrived at the restaurant and for a second Julienne was thrown off-guard at the opulence.

"Can we afford this?" she asked.

Cece laughed. "It's my treat."

Julienne bit her lip. Cece had said it was an apology, but this would be an expensive apology.

"C'mon," Cece said, impatient. "Think of it as a work dinner, if you want. I'm hungry."

Julienne nodded. Cece gave her name to the host and they were directed to a table near the window. The atmosphere was intimate, romantic, and in the brief silence as they sat down, Julienne found her gaze drifting to Cece's lips, imagining what it would be like to kiss them.

It felt like a date.

Again.

Julienne swallowed, tried to focus on the menu.

"Do you want wine? I don't mind if you do," Cece said.

"I don't think I should drink."

Cece hummed and didn't look up from her menu.

Julienne tried not to sigh.

The waiter took their orders and she sat back in her chair. She was pretty sure she wasn't dressed well enough for this restaurant, but Cece seemed completely at ease, as always.

"Do you want to talk about the other night?" Cece said quietly.

"You did say you owed me an apology," Julienne said.

Cece nodded, then set her jaw, looking resolved. "I'm sorry for ditching you to do coke."

"Why did you do it?" Julienne asked, more curious than anything.

"I mean... everyone does it," Cece said.

Julienne fought the urge to roll her eyes.

"I don't have a drug problem," Cece said. "I just do it sometimes at parties."

"What's the point in my being here if it's not gonna change anything about how you behave? Isn't that literally my job?"

"I have changed," Cece said. "It's only been a week and I haven't been late to work once."

"What if that girl you argued with had showed up?" Julienne asked. "Or what if you'd gotten caught? What if you'd stayed out till 6am because you were doing coke and having a great time, and then you didn't make it to work?"

"I know I screwed up, okay. You don't have to rub it in," Cece snapped.

"I just thought..." Julienne trailed off. "I thought I could trust you."

For the first time, Cece avoided making eye contact with her, looking down at the napkin folded on the table.

"I said I was sorry," she said, her voice small.

"What do you want me to do, Cece? I'm supposed to be here to help you."

Cece sighed. She was saved from answering, though, by the waiter approaching with their first course. They had both ordered salads to start, Cece's coming with some carefully-placed balls of buffalo mozzarella.

Cece didn't say anything until the waiter walked away.

"I don't have this figured out," she said, softly. "You are helping me."

Julienne took a bite of her salad. "We have to work together on this shit. If you get in trouble, so do I."

"I know," Cece said. "I guess I just thought..." she trailed off and took a bite of her salad.

Julienne waited, focusing on her own food.

"What did you think?" Julienne asked, eventually.

Cece shrugged. "I thought you'd give up on me, I guess. You were being so nice to me and I knew I didn't deserve it."

"What are you talking about?" Julienne asked. "Why wouldn't you deserve it?"

"C'mon," Cece said. "It's not like you haven't noticed I'm a disaster."

"So your place is a mess and you party," Julienne said. "I was like that when I was nineteen, too. Maybe not exactly like that, but I'm not perfect. Nobody is."

"You must have read the headlines," Cece said. "Most people don't have to hire someone to keep them out of trouble."

Julienne finished her salad and crossed her cutlery on the plate. "I feel like most people would have a friend who intervenes instead. I've only met your friends at parties."

"Joshua is a big teddy bear," Cece said. "He's chill, we

just hang out and get high together and it's relaxing instead of out of control."

Julienne bit her lip. "And Allie?"

Cece rolled her eyes. "Allie likes to party, and she likes her friends to party with her. She's not all bad."

"I don't think she liked me," Julienne said.

Cece gave a small smile. "She's protective. The girl I got in a fight with was my sorta-ex. She got mad I wouldn't come out and has been trying to prove she can have a better career as an out lesbian ever since. Allie was there for that whole thing. She looks out for me."

"Wow," Julienne said. "That's intense."

"Yeah," Cece said. "She didn't blackmail me, but we thought she might, for a bit. So Allie's a little difficult with new people."

They lapsed into silence as their plates were removed from the table, and then the main course arrived. Cece had ordered the salmon and Julienne had a spaghetti dish, and they smelled delicious.

Julienne twirled the spaghetti around her fork.

"It sounds really hard, not knowing who you can trust," she said to Cece, before taking her first bite.

Cece flinched. "I'm not lonely," she said defensively, even though that wasn't what Julienne had said. "I have friends. People look out for me."

"You have me," Julienne said, softly.

Cece looked up and met Julienne's eyes, and her cheeks turned slightly pink. "Do I?" Cece said.

Julienne dropped her fork and it clattered loudly in the otherwise quiet restaurant, and she flushed as she bent to collect it.

A waiter appeared with a clean one before she was even upright again.

Cece changed the subject, apparently done with talking about the other night, and Julienne supposed they'd resolved it, anyway. Cece hadn't promised not to do it again but... well, Julienne was hopeful.

She guessed they'd just have to take it day by day.

She had eaten half her plate of spaghetti without really noticing the flavor. She wasn't sure if that was a problem with the cooking or just her limited attention span. It was so easy to get lost in conversation with Cece. She felt a little bad for wasting her money on the expensive food, though. She didn't know when she'd get to eat food like that again.

Cece asked for the dessert menu, and seemed buoyed by the luxurious options, even making a specific suggestion for Julienne.

"What time do we have to be at the airport?" Julienne asked, after they'd ordered.

"We're on the last flight back," Cece said, checking the time on her phone. "I wanted to make sure we had time for a nice meal. If we leave in an hour, we'll be fine."

"Thank you for the meal," Julienne said. "Thank you for trying."

The butterflies in her stomach decided to make themselves known again. If this was a date, she found herself thinking, this would be the time she reached out across the table to hold Cece's hand.

But it wasn't a date.

They dawdled through their desserts. Julienne's strawberry soufflé was delicious, and the conversation between them was only a little stilted.

Cece didn't even blink at the number on the bill and whipped out her credit card. Julienne couldn't help but be envious of her attitude. She hadn't even got her first paycheck yet, she was still living off the last few dollars her parents had sent her.

It was just another way she and Cece were living in completely different universes.

It made her miss Tori and Reina and all her college friends a bit. It made her long for home.

NINETEEN

Their flight was cancelled. Julienne and Cece stood side by side, staring up at the departure board, in silence. The driver had already left.

Cece swore loudly, drawing a few glances from passersby.

"We'll just get another flight, right?" Julienne said.

Cece nodded, still looking up at the board as if willing it to change.

"I booked the last flight out," Cece said, her voice small. "I wanted to take you out to a nice meal so I got the latest one I could."

"Oh."

"I'm really sorry," Cece said. Her eyes were wide and a little desperate. "I don't know what we're going to do."

Julienne bit her lip. She hadn't expected Cece to be at such a loss. She slid into problem-solving mode, the same one she'd used when things had gone wrong in college, and took over from Cece.

She headed over to the airline desk, checking for alternative flights on her phone, and explained the situation to the steward.

He was sympathetic, but didn't have much in the way of good news. "I don't even have anything on any other flights in California, they're all fully booked. I can get you on one mid-morning tomorrow."

It didn't take much before Julienne had a plan in place. It wasn't ideal, but it was better than nothing. Once Julienne had explained she was travelling back from a photo-shoot with a magazine and she was someone's assistant, the steward seemed a little more willing to help them out.

Cece was fiddling with her phone as Julienne approached, looking anxious. She'd pulled a hat out of somewhere and tugged it down over her forehead, and Julienne wondered why until she realised that Cece was worried about being recognised.

"We're staying overnight," Julienne said. "But we've got rooms at a hotel, discounted, and there's a shuttle bus to take us there."

"A shuttle bus," Cece said, pulling a face.

"We can just get a cab, if you want," Julienne said. "Either way, we're staying here."

Cece nodded. "I'm sorry," she said. "I dragged you out here and now you're stuck with me."

"It's one night, it's not the end of the world," Julienne said. "Is there anyone other than Sadie I need to call?"

"I like it when you take charge," Cece said softly. It could have been innuendo, but Cece seemed shy as she said it, eyes cast downward. "No, Sadie can sort everything. I can do it, that's not your job."

Julienne shrugged. "I'm just trying to help."

"I know," Cece said, flashing her a quick smile. "Thank you."

Cece sent Sadie a text as they walked to the shuttle bus pick up.

"Where is this hotel?" Cece asked, looking at the bus schedule.

"It's on the strip, I think," Julienne said. "The airline said they had a deal with them."

Cece wrinkled her nose. "I can't believe I'm spending a night in Vegas and I can't drink or gamble at all."

"Come back when you're twenty-one," Julienne said. "I'm sure you'll enjoy it then."

"Does it bother you?" Cece asked. "That I'm underage, I mean."

"Why would it bother me?"

Cece raised an eyebrow and Julienne felt her cheeks heat up. She was saved from answering by the arrival of the shuttle bus.

They were the last to get on, surrounded by other tourists, and Cece pulled her cap low over her face. Julienne missed looking at her already, and she tried not to think about what that meant.

The shuttle dropped them on the strip outside their hotel. It wasn't Planet Hollywood, but it was pretty impressive, and crowded inside too. There were banners and signs everywhere for some kind of convention, directing people where they should sign in.

They headed for the front desk.

"We were sent here from the airport," Julienne said, and gave their names.

"Let me see," the clerk said.

"Our flight was cancelled," Cece said.

The clerk made a sympathetic noise, but it was clear they weren't really paying attention. "One double room?"

"Two rooms," Julienne said.

They shook their head. "We only have one. We're full up with the convention, you're lucky you got that one."

Julienne glanced at Cece, not sure what she was hoping to see.

"Let's just take it," Cece said. "If you're okay with that?" Her voice lilted up at the end and she shifted uneasily.

Julienne swallowed and nodded. She suspected Cece was even more tired than Julienne was, after their early start, and who knew if any other hotels would have room.

"Need a credit card and this form," the clerk said.

Cece passed over her card and filled out the form, and then they got a key and were on their way to the room. Julienne could feel a rising tide of anxiety in her stomach at the thought of sharing a bed with Cece.

Her phone buzzed with a text from Tori:

Hey J, I know ur working but are u gonna be back to watch Reina's tennis match? Starts at 10.30!

She swore.

"What's up?" Cece asked, sliding the keycard into the hotel door.

"My friend Reina has a tennis match today, it's her first televised competition. I was going to watch it with my roommate."

"We can watch it, if you want. Check and see if the TV has it."

"Are you sure? It might be boring."

Cece shrugged. "You've met my friends, it would be cool to see one of yours."

Julienne couldn't help but smile at that. "Okay," she said. "We should get snacks."

Cece laughed. "What channel is it, I'll see if they have it first."

Julienne told her while she texted Tori back, and Cece confirmed they had it.

It didn't start for more than an hour, though, so there was an awkward silence while they figured out what to do next.

"Do you want to go and see the fountains?" Julienne asked. "We've got some time to kill, and Vegas is prettier at night."

She couldn't help but feel a little excited at the thought of spending another evening with Cece, doing things they both enjoyed.

"I've only seen pictures," Cece said.

"It's better in person," Julienne said, confidently, as though she hadn't been drunk the whole time she was last there. "I'm sure we can walk from here."

It was almost as bright as day outside, with all the artificial light, and they walked slowly, taking in all the sights. The Bellagio Fountains weren't far, and they found a spot by the railing to wait for the show to start.

It began with a thunderous blast of bass and the fountains shooting straight up in the air, and beside her Cece let out a squeak and jumped. She moved an inch closer to Julienne, and Julienne held her breath. She was close enough that Julienne could feel her body heat.

She bit the inside of her cheek to keep from smiling.

The water dancing to the music was ethereal, and all the more powerful now that Julienne was watching it sober. The music was bass-heavy, a song Julienne recognised but couldn't name, and the effect was incredibly dramatic.

Cece whipped out her phone to take a photo.

"I was expecting like, boring classical music or something," Cece said.

"I think they change it up," Julienne said. "It was classical last time I was here."

"I forget you've done all this before," Cece said. "Is it really boring?"

Not with you, Julienne wanted to say. "I was drunk last time," she said, instead.

"Oh man, I bet this would be awesome stoned," Cece said.

Julienne didn't say anything.

"Sorry," Cece said. Julienne barely caught it over the music.

"You don't have to apologise for everything," Julienne said. "I'm not just standing here judging you all the time."

Cece smiled at her. "Okay," she said, looking pleased.

The show finished and they took a moment to catch their breath. It truly had been beautiful. They carried on walking down the strip, and Cece tapped on her phone, uploading the photo she'd taken earlier.

"I wonder who does the choreography for that," Cece wondered aloud.

"I never thought about it," Julienne said.

"I used to do dance training." Cece shrugged. "Just curious, that's all."

"I saw you in that music video when I went out with my friends," Julienne said. "My friend recognised you."

Cece laughed. "Is it killing you that you can't tell anyone we're—" she cut herself off abruptly, and looked away for just a second. "That we're working together?"

"You tagged me in that photo," Julienne reminded her, trying not to wonder what Cece had been about to say. "I had to tell my roommate I was your assistant."

They were on a more crowded part of the strip now, people handing out leaflets for events happening that evening. They ignored more than one person thrusting it directly in their face.

They paused by the fountains outside Caesar's Palace.

"Not nearly as impressive," Cece commented, and they were approached by another club promoter.

"Looking for a great night out, ladies?" he said, proffering a leaflet. "Cheap entry!"

"No, thanks," Cece said.

"Wait," he said. "I know you."

Cece made eye contact with Julienne. Julienne moved forward a little, trying to shut him out of their conversation, but the guy ignored her, pointing at Cece.

"You're Cece Browne! What are you doing tonight? You really want to come to this party, I'll throw in VIP for you, for free."

"She's underage," Julienne said, getting between the two of them.

He pushed at her, knocking her out of the way, and she lost her balance as the back of her knees hit the edge of the fountain.

It seemed to happen in slow motion as she fell backwards, hitting the surface of the water and plunging beneath it.

Jesus, it was cold.

Her clothes weighed her down, and it took a moment for her to get her bearings under water.

She surfaced to the sound of Cece swearing loudly at him. The water stank, and the bottom of the fountain was slick with algae, and she struggled to get her feet underneath her and stand upright. Her clothes felt heavy and her nose stung a little.

Cece turned around, ignoring the promoter, and

reached out to Julienne, pulling her up and out of the water with some effort.

Julienne was starting to shiver, and she didn't let go of Cece's hand once she was standing upright. She felt a little weak and completely ridiculous. A few people had stopped to look at the commotion.

"Please," she said to Cece. "Let's just go."

Cece looked like she wanted to chew the promoter out a little more, but he lifted his hands in defeat and walked away.

"Ugh, that guy," Cece said. "We should go back to the hotel, get you out of those clothes."

Julienne must have gone bright red, because Cece pulled a face.

"You're shivering, I mean," she said, quickly.

"This is so gross," Julienne said.

"Yeah, it stinks," Cece said. "What an asshole."

They made their way back to the hotel, Julienne moving a little slowly in her damp clothes. The Nevada heat helped, but not much. It wasn't until they were nearly back at the hotel that Julienne thought to check her phone.

"Shit, it's dead," she said. "It got soaked."

"Ugh!" Cece said, drawing the attention of someone passing by. "We should go back and make him pay for a new one."

"It was an accident," Julienne said, though she wasn't sure if that was true.

"Did you get one of his leaflets? We can call his boss, or something."

"I didn't."

"Me neither."

Inside the air conditioning of the hotel, the wet clothes

seemed to stick to Julienne's skin, and she started shivering again.

"I'm gonna ask if they have some rice we can put your phone in," Cece said. "Go up to the room and get changed, okay?"

Julienne took the key Cece offered her and rode the lift up to their floor. She didn't make eye contact with anyone, knowing she looked a mess. She felt gross, no longer dripping wet but still soaked through. Being freezing cold didn't help.

She found a robe on the back of the bathroom door and took her clothes off in there, worried about Cece walking in on her half way through. They were breaking enough workplace boundaries as it was, she didn't need to add that to the pile.

God, she hoped her clothes were dry by morning. It would be an unpleasant flight home, otherwise. She hung them near the A/C unit, hoping the airflow would help.

She took a shower to warm herself up and when she felt a bit more human, she got out and wrapped herself up in the robe. It was thick and soft against her skin, and she flicked on the TV and put it on mute in preparation for Reina's match. It would be starting soon.

She wished her phone was working so she could text Tori about it.

Cece knocked before she entered, carrying a Tupperware of dry rice.

"Put your phone in it," she said. "If it's still dead in the morning, I'll buy you a new one."

"You don't have to do that," Julienne said.

Cece shrugged. "If we can't track down the promoter, it's the next best thing. It wouldn't have happened if you weren't with me, anyways."

Julienne looked down, feeling her cheeks warm up. "Thanks," she said quietly.

"Is your friend on already?" Cece said, looking at the TV.

"Not yet. She's the next match."

"Perfect timing, then," Cece said. She looked at Julienne, sitting a little stiffly on the bed. "You look so cozy, I might put on a robe too."

"The robes are nice," Julienne said. It sounded like such an inane thing to say, as soon as she said it.

Cece nodded, making a decision, and disappeared into the bathroom. Julienne was just glad she didn't strip off right in front of her again.

Julienne unmuted the TV while she waited, and tried to think about it like a girls' night in. Just the two of them, hanging out and watching a tennis match.

It wasn't anything more than that, she told herself. It couldn't be.

TWENTY

It was a tense hour as they watched Reina play. Julienne had never seen her struggle so much before, and every serve she returned seemed hard-won. Julienne was chewing her lip in the final set, on edge as she watched Reina sweat and shout on the court.

She lost the match. It was kind of gutting to watch it end, to read the body language she was so familiar with through the screen.

Julienne wished she was by Reina's side, giving her a hug and a pep talk. It seemed so unfair that she was on the other side of the world.

"Can I borrow your phone?" Julienne asked, muting the TV.

"Sure," Cece said. "What for?"

"I just want to call Reina, give her some support."

Cece raised an eyebrow. "Where in the world is she?"

"The match was in China."

Cece rolled her eyes. "You're lucky I have international in my plan." She tossed Julienne her phone.

"Thank you," Julienne said. "I owe you."

"You fell into a fountain for me," Cece said. "Don't worry about it."

Julienne shot a text to Reina's number – she had it memorised – explaining her phone was broken and she loved her and if Reina needed someone to talk to, she could call.

Reina text back straight away:

i love you, call me!

Julienne hit the dial button and Reina picked up on the first ring.

"Hey, Ray," Julienne said.

"I blew it," Reina said. "It was a total disaster."

Julienne made a soothing noise. "I wish I could be there to give you a hug," she said. "It was one bad match. There'll be others. There's always others."

"You guys were all watching me embarrass myself," Reina said. "My first international match, and all my friends saw me lose."

"You made some amazing shots in there," Julienne said. "That serve in the second match was incredible. You blew her away."

"Not enough," Reina said.

"Hey," Julienne said. "Don't beat yourself up. Losses happen. Remember junior year, we didn't score a single point against UC Davis?"

"I remember," Reina said. She sounded tired.

"We made it to nationals the next year. There's always another chance to win."

Reina sighed. "I just feel like crap. I'm jet lagged and I don't know anyone here and it sucks. I miss you."

"I miss you too," Julienne said. "Though you'd kick my ass now. I would be a useless partner."

Reina laughed. "Next time I'm in LA, we'll book a court."

Julienne smiled at the thought. "Count on it," she said.

"I miss being part of such a small team," Reina said. "It's different competing at this level. We were like a family. It's not like that here."

"We also lived together," Julienne said. "That probably helped."

"I miss that, too," Reina said. "Ugh, can we talk about something else? I'm tired of tennis."

"Sure," Julienne said, easily. "What do you want to talk about?"

"Whose phone is this and where even are you?" Reina said. "Tori said you weren't watching with her. Do you have a hot date?"

"I'm in Vegas," Julienne said, looking out the window at the sparkling lights of the strip.

"What are you doing in Vegas?" Reina asked.

Julienne bit her lip, glanced back at Cece who was watching her on the bed. "I told you I got that job," she said. "But I can't tell you anything about it. It was just meant to be a day trip for a work thing, but then our flight got cancelled."

"Damn. A free night in Vegas? Why aren't you out making the most of it? You didn't have to stay in and watch me play."

"First of all, I always want to watch you play," Julienne said. "But I also fell into a fountain and got soaked. So my day hasn't exactly been a winner, either."

Reina laughed. "So you're there with your boss, or...?" she trailed off, clearly fishing for details.

"C'mon, Reina. You know what a non-disclosure agreement is, right? I can't tell you anything."

Reina sighed dramatically. "Here I am, your best friend, all alone on the other side of the world, and you won't tell me *anything*."

Julienne snorted. "My boss is watching me make this phone call," she said, glancing at Cece again. "My lips are sealed. Permanently."

"So unfair," Reina said.

"I wish I could tell you everything," Julienne said. "But you know I've never been a rule-breaker."

"God, you and your rules," Reina said. "You were so neurotic before Nationals."

Julienne laughed.

Reina sighed. "Hey, I should go. I have tournament stuff to do. Thank you for calling, I needed this. Love you."

"Love you too, Ray."

Julienne hung up the phone and passed it back to Cece.

"I hate it when you call me your boss," Cece said. "I am not anyone's boss."

Julienne laughed. "It's hard to explain who you are to Reina without giving it away. I take that non-disclosure seriously."

"Thanks," Cece said. "I mean, Sadie would sue your ass if you went to the press with something, but I appreciate it, anyway."

"Your secrets are safe with me," Julienne said.

Cece smiled at her. "What about your secrets?"

"I don't have any secrets," Julienne said, "and nobody cares about me, anyway."

"I care about you," Cece said softly. "I can tell you're a really good friend, too. I bet Reina needed to hear from you."

Julienne felt her face getting warm. "We have each

other's back. Doubles partners and roommates, we've got a lot of history."

"Let me compliment you," Cece said. "You're a good friend, and a good person."

"Thanks," Julienne said awkwardly. She was still standing stiffly by the bed, looking down at Cece.

Cece picked at a loose thread on the dressing gown, her voice going a little quiet. "I thought you were just being nice to me because you had to."

"I'm not," Julienne said.

"I know," Cece said. "I'm sorry I'm such a dick sometimes. I do know you're only trying to help."

Julienne didn't know what to say. She sat down on the bed, cross-legged, facing Cece.

"I like you," Cece carried on. "I'm sorry for pushing you away."

"I'm not going anywhere," Julienne said.

Cece sighed. "I don't know if I believe you."

Julienne waited.

"People always give up on me when shit gets hard," Cece said. "Sadie is like, my third manager since my mom died."

"That sucks," Julienne said softly.

"I trust you," Cece said. "I'm not sure I should, yet, but I do."

Julienne swallowed. "I'm glad," she said. "We're in this together."

Cece lifted her chin and met Julienne's eyes. "I really like being in this with you," she said, her eyes wide and vulnerable.

Julienne felt something bloom in the empty space in her chest.

"We make a good team," Julienne said, her mouth a little dry. She fought the urge to lick her lips.

Cece furrowed her brow and sat up on the bed, shifting a little closer. "More than that," she said. "I just- I really like you, Julienne."

Julienne swallowed.

She didn't know what to think. She didn't dare hope Cece was saying what she thought she was saying. It was crossing that careful boundary that Julienne had been clinging to.

But there was a tiny kernel of hope in her heart regardless.

"Julienne?"

Her heartbeat pounded in her ears as Cece shifted closer on the bed.

"Can I kiss you?"

She didn't know how Cece managed to shrink the space between them. She didn't know when she moved to be closer to Cece. They were so close Julienne could feel her breath against her lips.

Her gut twisted in knots. "Yes," she said, her voice a little hoarse.

It was gentle at first, when their lips met. They pressed against each other, just a brush of skin on skin, for a brief, wonderful moment, before it deepened into something with a little more heat.

Julienne wanted to gasp for air. She opened her mouth and Cece's opened with it, and somehow there was a hand on the nape of her neck, one of hers wrapped around Cece's back.

They stayed connected as they tilted sideways, and then they were horizontal on the bed, their bodies flush against each other. Their noses knocked together clumsily, but it didn't matter, it was perfect.

She lost herself in the kiss. It felt like all the tension from the last few days had finally unfurled, and all of it had been building to this moment in a hotel bed in Las Vegas. It couldn't be more perfect.

It was as though they were on a different planet altogether to that night at the party.

The press of Cece's lips against her own was so intense it was almost suffocating, and their bare legs rubbing against each other was a reminder that neither of them were fully clothed. It would be so easy to untie Cece's robe, to touch every inch of her.

Her fingers tingled with temptation.

She opened her eyes and broke the kiss. Seeing Cece's face up close like this, being able to count her eyelashes and the spaces between her freckles, it was – she didn't know what it was.

Her heart soared.

Neither of them said anything, just the breath moving between them. They were both breathing harder than they should have been.

It was Julienne who broke first, unable to keep looking into Cece's rich brown eyes. She pressed her forehead to Cece's shoulder, feeling the soft texture of the robe against her skin.

They were still holding each other like life rafts in that vast hotel bed.

"You okay?" Cece said softly.

Julienne lifted her head up. "Yeah," she said. "I've been telling myself this is a bad idea all week, though."

Cece laughed, but it was soft, gentle.

"I do a lot of stupid things," she said, "but I don't think this was one of them."

The press of Cece's lips on her cheek was so quick she barely felt it, like a butterfly landing on her skin for an instant, and then Cece moved away.

Julienne missed her immediately.

"What happens next?" she asked.

"I don't know," Cece said. "I just wanted you to know I liked you."

"Message received," Julienne said, a little awkwardly.

Cece gave a soft little snort. "You're interesting. You're not like anyone I've ever met before."

"Really?"

Cece gave a one-shouldered shrug, resting her head on the pillow as her eyes searched Julienne's face. "Like I said, I trust you. You're a good person."

"I don't find myself very interesting," Julienne said, voice going hoarse again. She felt like the honesty was pulled from her throat by Cece's steady gaze.

Cece shrugged again. She looked so relaxed and comfortable when Julienne felt wire-strung, like the kiss had electrified something in her.

"Different perspectives," Cece said.

"I don't understand you," Julienne said, softly.

"Stop thinking so much," Cece said. She stretched, and the robe gaped a little, showing her cleavage. In a quieter voice, she said: "You understand me better than most people."

"I'm trying," Julienne said, giving her a small smile.

Cece smiled back at her, her face so open it almost hurt to look at. It was completely different to the other smiles she'd seen Cece wear, at work, at parties, on social media.

It was just for her.

"Stop thinking so much," Cece said, and pressed closer to her again. The TV was still on mute in the background, but Julienne didn't know or care where the remote was. She just wanted to feel Cece's skin against her own again, to twine their fingers together.

Cece kissed her, her leg slipping between Julienne's.

Julienne put her hand on the tie of Cece's robe, then pulled back. "Is this okay?" she said.

Cece nodded, and Julienne kissed her again, untying Cece's robe and moving her hand underneath, feeling the warmth of Cece's body and the softness of her skin.

"Tickles," Cece said, against Julienne's mouth. "Are you sure you want to do this?"

Julienne swallowed. "Maybe we should slow down," she said. That seemed like the sensible thing to say, and being sensible put Julienne on familiar ground. Things were complicated enough already.

Cece nodded. "That's probably a good idea," she said.

"It's late," Julienne said. "We got up early."

Cece shifted on the bed, sitting up so she could move her robe out from underneath her and toss it to the floor. She was still wearing her underwear, but it made Julienne's throat dry to see all her bare skin like that, to be allowed to look at her lithe curves.

Cece smirked at her.

Julienne swallowed.

Cece flicked off the TV.

"Are you tired?" Cece asked.

Julienne nodded. She dropped her robe to the floor and slid under the covers before she could feel self conscious.

The bed was already warm from Cece's body heat, and Julienne lay on one side, facing Cece.

Cece turned the light off. For a moment, the only sound in the dark room was the two of them breathing.

Then, breaking the silence: "Can I touch you?"

Julienne could hear the blood rushing in her ears. "Yes," she said, her voice soft.

It began with just the brush of fingertips on Julienne's arms, leaving a path of flames as they travelled down to her wrist. Then, touching her hip over her underwear, then further down the outside of her thigh.

Goosebumps rippled over Julienne's skin. She'd dated, she'd had sex, but just the lightest of touches from Cece was more intimate than anything she'd felt before.

She reached out under the covers, feeling blindly in the dark, until her thumb brushed Cece's shoulder. Julienne hadn't considered that touching a shoulder could feel so charged, but Cece's skin was soft beneath her hand and Julienne wanted to explore every inch of it.

Her eyes adjusted to the dim light of the room as her hand travelled around Cece's torso, the curve of her waist and the smooth planes of her back.

Cece's eyes drifted shut.

Julienne pressed her lips to Cece's collarbone, neck, nose.

"You're perfect," she murmured.

Cece snorted. "We both know that's not true."

It didn't matter. In that gentle, fragile moment, she was perfect.

TWENTY-ONE

Sunlight streaming through a crack in the curtains woke Julienne before her alarm. It took her a moment to remember where she was: curled in Cece's arms, her weight a solid warmth behind her.

She could feel Cece's chest rising and falling behind her, and her heart fluttered.

She pressed a careful kiss to Cece's wrist and slid out from beneath it, leaving Cece to sprawl further across the bed. The only clothes she had looked worse for wear, and didn't smell great either, but she dressed anyway. She opened the room service menu, in case Cece wanted breakfast, but the price was higher than she was expecting and she didn't want to add to the hotel bill. Not when she knew Cece would be paying for it.

She felt even more uncomfortable about the ease with which Cece offered her things now that they'd spent the night together. She was sure, if Julienne asked, Cece would hand over her credit card for whatever.

God, she was in so much trouble.

Cece looked so peaceful as she slept, drooling a little in a way Julienne should have found gross.

Part of her wanted to go back to bed and stay there, the whole day, with Cece.

She wondered if the hotel had a gym. If she couldn't tell her friends what had happened, she could at least pound out some miles on a treadmill, get her head in order. She didn't know what to think.

The weight of the non-disclosure agreement felt heavy on her chest.

Julienne turned her phone on, relieved it powered on without any issue. She had some texts from Tori and the tennis group chat had been active too, watching Reina's match.

She sent Tori a text saying she'd been stranded in Vegas and she'd watched the match, just to keep her updated. She jumped a little when Cece's alarm went off, and tried to look relaxed, casual.

"Thought you ditched me," Cece said, voice rough from sleep.

Julienne laughed, a little awkwardly. "Just an early riser," she said.

"Gross. How long do we have?"

"A while," Julienne said. "I wasn't sure if you wanted breakfast?"

Cece shook her head. "Coffee would be great, though."

Julienne filled the coffee maker up with water and a pod and flicked it on.

"Can you do me a favor?" Cece asked.

Julienne looked up at her. "Depends," she said. She kept her tone easy, but she was sure Cece recognised the wariness in it.

Cece's nose twitched. "Don't tell Sadie about last

night?" She paused, seemingly uncertain. "Not yet, anyways."

Julienne filled a cup with coffee and passed it to Cece before answering.

"Is it okay that I still work for you?"

"I like working with you," Cece said. "You work for Sadie, not me. I'm not your boss."

"Why do you want to lie to her?"

"It's not lying," Cece said. "Just, like, omission."

Julienne was pretty sure that was just a subcategory of lying.

"I don't want things to get complicated," Cece said, voice turning pleading. "And anyway, she'll definitely fire you. I don't want that for either of us."

Julienne nodded. She hated that her job depended on a lie, hated that she'd put herself in this position. "Okay," she said, but the word tasted sour in her mouth.

"Ugh, speak of the devil," Cece said, looking at her phone.

She answered it, and Julienne busied herself making another cup of coffee.

"You know I hate it when you start a phone call with 'don't panic, everything's under control'," Cece said.

Julienne's heart stopped for a moment.

"Oh, fuck," Cece said. It sounded heartfelt. "I'll tell her. Do you think they'll be at the airport?"

Julienne stirred her coffee. She wished Cece could just put it on loudspeaker.

"I don't want to lock down my socials," Cece said. "It's not my fault- okay. Okay."

Julienne took a sip of her coffee. She knew it wouldn't settle her nerves but she hoped, regardless.

"Don't put out a statement. I'll tell her. Thanks, Sadie."

She ended the call, and Julienne waited.

"Bad news," Cece said. "I don't know how it happened, but someone took photos of us at the restaurant last night."

"What kind of photos?"

"It looked like a date, I guess," Cece said. "That's the story they're selling, anyways."

Julienne's cheeks flushed. It had felt like a date, but she didn't know that she wanted the whole world to know that.

"You should put your socials on private," Cece said. "I'll untag you in that photo."

Julienne nodded, tapping buttons on her phone without really thinking about it. There were already comments coming in from people she didn't recognise, and she hated it.

"I need to turn off the comments," she said.

She glanced up to see Cece biting her lip. "I can just delete the photo," she said. "I'm so sorry. This is bullshit."

Julienne didn't know what to say. It *was* bullshit.

Cece sighed. "Can you say something, please?"

"I don't know what to say," Julienne said. "This is your wheelhouse, not mine."

Cece nodded. "The airport might suck. I don't know if there will be cameras there, but probably."

Julienne shut her eyes. She hadn't thought about there being paparazzi there. "What should I do?"

Julienne felt a little numb as she listened to Cece giving tips on how to hide your face. She couldn't believe this was what she was listening to, that this was what her life had become.

"What does Sadie think?" she asked, eventually.

Cece frowned. "She's not happy. She's drafted a statement, but I don't want her to release it yet. She thinks maybe the magazine interview had something to do with the story."

"Are you sure we shouldn't tell her the truth?" Julienne asked. "Won't it be easier if she knows?"

Cece shook her head. "She'll say it's time for me to come out. She'll make us into a story she has to sell. It's just us, right? I just want to enjoy it."

Julienne bit her lip. It wasn't as simple as that, and she had a feeling Cece knew that.

"Are you going to read the story?" Julienne asked. "The one about us."

Cece shook her head. "Nothing in it is gonna be true, there's no point."

Julienne looked down at the dregs in her coffee mug. Everything had been turned upside down by one phone call. She didn't know which way was up anymore; she couldn't see a path out of this.

"Julienne," Cece said softly. "It's gonna be okay, we'll figure it out."

"How are you always so sure?" Julienne asked.

Cece shrugged. "I've survived far worse rumours than dating a beautiful woman."

Julienne flushed. It was easy to get lost in Cece's eyes, her easy smile, the memory of her plush lips.

God, she was so far gone.

Cece called them a cab, not wanting to ride the shuttle bus again, and then that morning-after unease settled in the room.

"Are you going to put some clothes on?" Julienne asked.

Cece snorted. "We're not leaving just yet," she said. "What's the rush?"

"You're really distracting," Julienne said, her cheeks flushing red.

Cece crossed the room and invaded Julienne's personal space. She framed Julienne's face with her cupped hands. "I should hope so," she said. "Good morning."

Julienne tipped her chin to meet Cece's lips for a brief kiss.

"Your breath stinks," Cece said.

"So does yours."

Cece shrugged and lifted her chin to kiss Julienne again. In the back of her mind, she wondered why Cece was okay with her bare skin touching Julienne's grimy clothes, but her thoughts were swept away by the warmth of Cece's body against hers and the bare skin beneath her fingertips.

"I like kissing you," Cece said, when they broke for air.

Julienne just blinked at her. For all that Cece was erratic and confusing, she always said whatever she was feeling. There were no masks, no platitudes.

Julienne didn't even know if she could put her feelings into words. Cece seemed to be able to make sense of her like no one else could.

Cece stepped away from her and grabbed her shirt, and Julienne couldn't stop looking at her lips, flushed pink and shiny with saliva. She was more distracted by Cece than she'd ever been.

"You're staring," Cece said. Julienne could hear the smirk in her voice.

Julienne flushed hot again. "Sorry," she said.

Cece turned to face her, pulling on her pants. "You can't look at me like that in public, okay? We have to look like we're just friends."

Julienne swallowed. "Right," she said, a little stiffly. "Sorry."

Cece gave her a small smile. "I'm sorry, too," she said. "You ready?"

Julienne nodded, grabbing her handbag and heading for the lift. She tried to keep her mind on staying professional, but her job, her whole life, seemed to revolve around Cece.

It was hard to forget the shape of her in Julienne's arms.

Julienne watched as Cece signed the bill without really looking at it. She tried to quell the pang of anxiety that came with it. Another reminder that at only nineteen, Cece's life was completely different to Julienne's.

They walked in step out the automatic doors, but they were met with a cacophony of bright lights and noise.

"Did you spend the night together?" someone shouted.

"Is this the first girl you've fucked?" yelled someone else.

Julienne couldn't breathe. She didn't know how many of them there were, but she felt trapped, closed in. They were all holding cameras at eye level, yelling words she couldn't make out.

She'd forgotten everything Cece had told her in the hotel. She felt rooted to the spot, paralyzed by the attention. She just looked at Cece, feeling panic rise in her chest. Frustration was written all over Cece's face.

"C'mon," Cece said, holding one arm out to push through the crowd as she grabbed Julienne's arm with the other.

Her hand was an iron grip around Julienne's wrist as she pulled her through the crowd. Mercifully, the taxi was already waiting for them, and Cece shoved her in first, then piled in after her. Julienne slid along the seat as Cece slammed the door shut.

She buried her head in her hands. Cameras flashed behind her head, and the taxi didn't move. Julienne could still hear them yelling.

"Go, please," Cece said. "To the airport."

It wasn't until the car started moving that Cece looked up at her. "Are you okay?"

Julienne nodded mutely. Nausea rolled in her stomach.

"Seatbelts," said the taxi driver.

Julienne obeyed. She felt like she was watching herself from a distance. She wondered how she'd looked through the lens of a camera.

She thought she might throw up.

"I bet it was that club promoter or something," Cece muttered. "What an asshole."

Was this what it was like to be famous? Never knowing when your privacy would be violated, your space invaded?

"I'm sorry," Cece said. "I didn't think they'd be at the hotel. Sadie didn't either, she just said look out at the airport. We could have left out a back exit, or something."

Julienne stared out the window, looking for escape in the endless lights of Vegas. She hadn't expected it to be so intense, or to have affected her so much.

"Julienne?" Cece said softly.

"That was horrible," Julienne said.

"She speaks," Cece said, giving her a small smile. "I've got a baseball cap you can wear if you want."

"Don't you need it?"

Cece shrugged. "Not if you do," she said, like it was the easiest thing in the world.

"I'm nobody," Julienne said. "I'm just me. I don't matter. Why do they think I matter?"

"You matter to me," Cece said, her voice so soft it made Julienne's chest ache. "They think they can embarrass me, us, and that people will want to read about it. That's all. It's a story they can sell."

"That's terrible."

Cece gave her a half smile. "It is what it is."

"Is it worth it?" Julienne asked.

"Is what worth it?"

"Fame," Julienne said. "The money, the acting career, whatever you're in this for."

Cece shrugged. "It's just what I've always known," she said. She glanced at the taxi driver, clearly worried about being overheard. "I never had anything I wanted to protect before," she said.

Julienne swallowed.

"Cap?" Cece asked, as their cab pulled up to the airport.

Julienne shook her head. "Nobody knows what I look like if you're not beside me."

"Point," Cece said. She put the hat on and tugged it low over her face. "Do you want to split up?"

Julienne thought about facing the paparazzi alone, even if they wouldn't recognise her, and something inside of her seized up. She shook her head.

Cece nodded and paid the taxi driver, then pulled her hood up over her head.

"They'll be inside, probably," Cece said, once they were out of the cab. "That's usually where they are at LAX."

Julienne blinked in the bright sun.

Cece grabbed her hand and gave it a squeeze. "C'mon, let's rip off the band-aid. There's no use dragging it out."

Julienne looked down at their joined hands. Cece followed her gaze and dropped her hand, and Julienne wondered why she felt so empty inside, suddenly.

She didn't know how much space to put between them. Spending the night wrapped up in Cece had warped everything somehow, like she didn't know how to be her friend anymore.

"Are you okay?"

"You don't have to keep asking," Julienne said.

She couldn't read the expression on Cece's face in the shadow of her cap. She started walking, wanting to get this over with.

Julienne just wanted to go home and get changed out of these awful clothes.

Cece kept pace with her, staying a careful arms length apart. Julienne missed having the solid reassurance of Cece by her side, but she didn't know who was watching, and that was the scariest part. Julienne hadn't signed up for fame, for being watched, for people posting photos of her online.

She'd never wanted to be famous.

Julienne kept her head down as they walked to the check-in desk, repeating Cece's tips from the hotel room that morning in her head. She tried to ignore the flash of the camera and the people shouting Cece's name. They were less crude than the ones outside the hotel, at least.

"Is this what your life is like?" she asked, as Cece handed her a boarding pass.

Cece didn't answer, just led her through security until they were through to the safety of the first class lounge.

"Most of the time nobody notices me," Cece said. "I'm not that famous."

"Famous enough," Julienne said.

Cece shrugged, settling into the seats. "It's too late to opt out now."

Something uneasy settled in Julienne's gut.

It wasn't too late for Julienne to opt out.

TWENTY-TWO

Julienne tried to distract herself with a book for most of the flight home, as Cece napped beside her. It was hard not to steal glances at her, to wonder what it was like to be able to sleep so easy after being harassed like that.

Everything about it felt wrong. Julienne was putting her whole life at risk for a job she wasn't even doing very well. She cared about Cece, but she wasn't sure that was enough to take that kind of public scrutiny.

They went straight to Sadie's office from the airport, through a thick crowd of paparazzi, and dread lined Julienne's throat like acid.

"We're not telling her about last night," Cece said. "Trust me, it's easier that way."

Julienne wanted to argue, but Cece was already out of the lift and waving hello to the receptionist. Julienne trailed behind as she headed straight for Sadie's office. She hoped she didn't look as anxious as she felt.

Sadie looked the picture of composure, and Julienne regretted even more not insisting Cece let her go home and change.

"I'm sorry about this," Sadie said, speaking directly to Julienne. "You shouldn't have been caught out like that, and I know it's only your first week on the job. It's a lot to handle."

Julienne tried to conjure up a professional response, but words failed her.

"It's been a rough 24 hours," Cece said. "Some club promoter pushed her in the fountain because he wanted me to come to his party."

Sadie frowned. "Maybe I need to get you a proper security escort."

"No," Cece said.

"Why not?" Julienne asked.

Cece met Julienne's eyes, challenge written in her face. "One person with me is fine. I don't want a whole entourage following me around."

"Alright," Sadie said. "But you need to lay low for a while. No meals together, no public events. Just for a week or two, until they move on to the next story."

"I'm tired of the rumours," Cece said. "Do you think this is Leah's fault? She's told the press we used to be a thing, or something?"

"I don't know what caused it," Sadie said. "I know you don't want to come out. I'm not pressuring you to do anything. But I do think if we get ahead of this, it won't happen again. They want it to be a gotcha moment."

"I'm thinking about it, I promise," Cece said. "I just don't want to draw any more attention to Julienne."

"We need to come up with a plan for the next time this happens," Sadie said. "Next time, it actually might be someone you're dating. I want a timeline."

"I can't tell the world before telling my mom," Cece said, her eyes a little wide. She looked away from Sadie and

Julienne wondered if she was trying not to cry. "And she's dead. So," She finished flatly, not looking at either of them.

"I'm sorry for pushing," Sadie said, though she didn't look entirely satisfied. "For now, lay low for a few days. Separately or together, I don't mind. Work and nowhere else, Cece."

Cece nodded. "I think Julienne deserves a few days off," she said.

Julienne gave her a small smile.

"I'm glad you're getting on, at least," Sadie said, hands steepled in front of her. "Alright. It'll blow over, Julienne, don't worry. I'll try to stop them from finding out your personal details, but it might be too late for that."

Julienne's gut twisted. "Thanks," she said. She wondered if she should worry about the paparazzi showing up at her door, or following her car.

If there was ever a time to tell Sadie the truth of the situation, it was now. She hated lying like this.

"Well," Sadie said. "Call if you have any problems."

With that, they were dismissed. There was an awkward silence as they waited for the lift.

"You're really quiet," Cece said eventually, bouncing on her heels a little.

"It's been an intense day," Julienne said, not meeting her eyes. "I just want to go home."

There was a ding as the lift door opened and they stepped inside.

"Talk to me," Cece said, softly.

Cece's face was so open, so ready to listen, that it hurt Julienne to look at her. "It's been a really emotional day," Julienne said. She sighed. "I hate lying to Sadie. She *should* fire me."

"I think you're doing a great job," Cece said.

Julienne snorted.

"It's complicated, but we'll figure it out." Cece reached out to grab her hand. Their fingers brushed and then Julienne moved away, putting space between them in the confined space.

The lift doors opened.

"I'm sorry," Julienne said. "Today was just... awful. I want to go home."

"Can I give you a ride, at least?"

Julienne nodded. She didn't know how to feel.

She sat, mutely, in the passenger seat of Cece's car, and was oddly pleased to find Cece needed directions to her apartment. It meant they didn't have to talk about anything else.

Maybe it meant Cece didn't know her as well as she thought she did, either.

"You can text me, anytime," Cece said, when she pulled up to Julienne's building. "Like, we could just hang out at my place and watch a movie or something. I'll be bored stuck at home."

Julienne opened her mouth, then closed it again.

Something that looked like hurt flickered across Cece's face, and then she opened her mouth to speak again.

"I'll text you," Julienne said, and got out of the car, before Cece could say anything else.

She felt like an asshole. She hadn't even asked if Cece was okay.

Her legs were leaden as she climbed the stairs to her apartment. Tori was out, at least, so she didn't have to explain anything. She tossed her phone on charge, ignoring the messages from the group chat that lit up. She didn't want to know if anyone had seen anything about her and Cece on Twitter or anywhere else.

She didn't want to know anything, really. She thought it might be nice to forget the world existed for a bit.

She stepped into the shower, hoping to wash off what it had felt like to have all those eyes on her, to hear them speculate about her sex life.

She pressed her forehead against the cool tile. How did Cece live like this? Constantly dancing on the edge of being the butt of some magazine's joke, for being too loud or too queer or too messy?

Julienne didn't know if she could live like that. If that was the price of admission for being involved with Cece, she wasn't prepared to pay it. She wasn't sure it mattered if Cece came out or not. She would still be famous, and people cared about who she was dating.

Cece was beautiful, and charismatic, and surprisingly kind, and there was something about her that Julienne couldn't look away from. She was so drawn to Cece that it terrified her.

It terrified her that she was doing things she'd never otherwise do: hooking up in a Vegas hotel, lying to her boss, getting drunk at work. Being around Cece was intoxicating, overpowering.

It made her feel alive.

She stood in the shower, feeling empty, for who knew how long. She hated that she was trapped in this situation without anyone to ask for advice. There was no one to tell, to vent to, to egg her on in sending that risqué text. It was just her and Cece, making bad decisions together.

She put on her pyjamas after she showered even though it was only early afternoon, then she tossed the rest of her clothes in the wash. It was strange, even the clothes she'd worn in her week with Cece were different, like she was dressing up as a different person.

A shiver ran down her spine.

Her phone vibrated on the desk where she'd left it.

A text from Cece flashed up on the screen, and Julienne tried to ignore the thrill that ran through her at the idea that Cece was at home, alone, thinking of her.

Cece: Your books from the other day are still at mine :) I can bring them over if u want to read on ur day off?

Julienne put her phone back on the table, face down.

The text was a pretty blatant excuse for Cece to come over, and Julienne wanted to give in. She wanted to get swept up in Cece and let her run away with her heart, forget that Julienne was supposed to be reining her in.

It wasn't a good idea for either of them. She felt guilty about it, after the look on Cece's face in Sadie's office. She thought Cece might need her right now, but Julienne needed to be alone more.

When they were together, Julienne got lost in Cece. The paparazzi had brought her down to earth with a bump, but she didn't know where to go from there.

She felt like a delicate house of cards that could fold at any moment, and the only thing keeping her together was not thinking about it.

TWENTY-THREE

It was dark outside when her phone vibrating on her desk woke her up. She'd gone to bed early after watching a movie with Tori, and her brain was foggy with sleep.

Cece, ringing her at 2am. That spelled trouble.

She flicked the light on as she answered.

"Hey, Cece, is everything okay?"

"Hey Jules," Cece said, her voice a little breathy. "Everything is great. How are you?"

"I'm fine," Julienne said carefully. "You're up late."

"Josh came over," Cece said. "He wanted to show solidarity. We had some drinks."

Julienne was glad Cece couldn't see her rolling her eyes.

"You didn't text me back," Cece said, her voice small.

"Sorry," Julienne said. "I was really tired, I guess. Are you drunk?"

"A little," Cece said. She paused. "I miss you. Is that weird?"

"It's a little weird, since I saw you earlier today," Julienne said. "Aren't you tired? It's been such a long day."

"Tired is relative," Cece said, and Julienne could

picture her giving that dismissive flick of the wrist. "I just wanted to talk to you."

Something in Julienne's chest tightened. "What do you want to talk about?" she said.

"I don't know," Cece said. "Your voice sounds different on the phone."

Julienne cleared her throat, feeling self-conscious. "I hope you're not working tomorrow," she said.

Cece laughed, but it was short and sharp and sounded false. "Do you ever stop worrying? I'm not, it's fine."

"It's my job to worry," Julienne said. "Remember?"

"Yeah, you're great at that," Cece said. "But Sadie gave you the day off, so you can relax."

Julienne clenched her fists. She hated people telling her to relax, like it was that easy, like worrying wasn't part of who she was. "It's not that simple," she said.

Cece made a 'huh' noise that Julienne couldn't interpret without seeing her face. "Is this a bad time or something?"

"I was asleep," Julienne said. "I'm just not really in the mood for this, right now."

She knew she was being snippy, but she couldn't help it. She was *tired*, and she hadn't expected to have to deal with drunk Cece on the phone tonight.

She wanted a day off. She was starting to realise that with Cece, there were no days off.

"Why don't you just chill out, relax?" Cece asked. "Smoke some weed, drink some wine, whatever suits you."

Julienne hated being told to relax. She knew she could be a little overcautious, a little uptight. She didn't need Cece to point it out, to pressure her to get drunk to change something about herself.

She thought Cece liked her for who she was.

"Did you call me just to tell me to relax?" Julienne asked.

"No, but you're killing my fun drunk buzz. Don't you ever need to unwind? Take a day off from being uptight."

"I unwind," Julienne said. She felt stiff, her words sounding stale even to her own ears. She hated being called uptight. She hated everything about this conversation.

There was a long pause.

Cece broke the silence, changing tack: "I do want to meet your friends. I want to meet Reina. She seems so cool."

"She's pretty busy," Julienne said, feeling uneasy. Everyone who met Julienne first, then Reina, always liked Reina more. She was the fun one, after all. "She doesn't come to LA much."

"We should have a party, invite all our friends. I bet it would be amazing," Cece said, her words slurring.

Julienne shut her eyes. "I don't think that's a good idea," she said.

Cece sighed. "Do you ever have fun ideas?"

Julienne felt tears welling up in her eyes. Cece was just drunk, drunk and a little mean. It cut too close to the bone of all of Julienne's insecurities.

"I think I'm going to be sick," Cece said.

"Drink some water," Julienne said. "Have you eaten?"

"You're doing it again," Cece said.

"This is my job, Cece," Julienne reminded her.

Cece barked out a sharp laugh. "Right," she said. "Your job."

"Cece..." Julienne trailed off.

"Goodnight, Jules," Cece said, and hung up.

Julienne looked at her phone in her hand. She didn't know what to do. She didn't know how to talk to Cece when she was like this, and maybe it would have been easier if Cece's words didn't have the sting of truth in them.

She was the boring one. She'd been hired to be boring.

Who could blame Cece for wanting more excitement in her life? She had glamorous parties and people who cared about who she was dating, what her next project was.

Julienne's life felt pretty empty compared to that. The paparazzi intruding for one, exhausting morning had thrown her whole world off-kilter, but that was Cece's normal.

They were too different. The phone call, at least, made that clear.

Julienne turned the light off and tried to go back to sleep, but anxious nausea stirred in her stomach. She cared about Cece's opinion too much. She cared about being seen as boring, or uptight, or a buzzkill, even though that was her job.

It hurt to think about Cece seeing her that way.

God, she needed this job. She needed to not be falling for Cece, so she could do her damn job. She needed everything to make sense again, and to not have instructions from her boss to stay home, out of sight.

She lay awake turning the problem over and over in her mind, finding no way out.

She must have drifted off eventually, woken abruptly by her alarm going off at its usual time. She still hadn't decided what to do, what to say to Cece.

She had half packed her gym bag and was getting ready to go run off some of her stress when she realised there was a decent chance she would bump into Cece there. She didn't know what Cece had planned for her day off, especially since she was probably hungover, but going to the gym had been in her calendar.

She put her gym bag down. Maybe she'd go for a run, she thought, knowing she wouldn't.

Pacing inside the apartment satisfied the itch to move, but she still felt a little trapped. She was used to her gym routine, to moving her body every day of the week, and between Vegas and now this, she had so much pent up energy.

She felt stuck. All her bad decisions had her trapped in a corner, and now she couldn't even leave her apartment. It was worse than being unemployed.

If she hadn't listened to Reina and taken this job, she might be living a completely different life right now.

She typed out a text to Reina, then deleted it, thinking of the careful wording of the non-disclosure agreement. She paced through the whole apartment, did all of the dishes.

She didn't reach out to Cece, not wanting to know if her mood had improved. If she texted her and Cece told her she was uptight and boring, she thought she might crumble.

When her phone vibrated she felt dread curdle in her stomach.

If it was Cece, she had no idea what she would say.

It wasn't, and she breathed a sigh of relief before she registered who it was actually from. The Carter Gallery, the bombed interview that had started this whole mess, had reached out.

Dear Julienne

I wanted to reach out to you to inform you that we have had another opening at the gallery that we need to fill urgently. It is a lower-level position than the one you originally applied for, and compensated accordingly, but the team discussed it and we felt you would be a good fit. I've attached the job description for your perusal.

Please could you give me a call today and let me know if you are still available.

Best wishes,

Madison

Julienne nearly dropped her phone. Her hands trembled as she downloaded the attached pdf, then she tossed her phone aside and switched on her laptop. Maybe if it was on her computer screen it would seem more real.

It wasn't the job she'd applied for, but it might just solve all of her problems.

It would barely be working in an art gallery, it was mostly busywork and answering phone calls. It was better than nothing, and a lot closer to her dream job than working with Cece was.

It meant she could stay in LA without all of Cece's complications.

It would be a mistake to say no, she told herself. It had landed in her lap. She'd never have to worry about the paparazzi again, or any of the other curveballs Cece was prone to throwing her way. She wouldn't have to face her and let out all the hurt she'd felt during that drunk phone call.

She took a deep breath and read it over a second time.

Reina would tell her to do it, just like she'd told her to take the job with Cece.

That decided her. She typed Madison's number into her phone, her hands trembling as she did.

Maybe she was being a little overeager, calling as soon as she got the email, but the phone was already ringing and it was too late for second thoughts now.

Her heart pounded.

"Carter Gallery, Madison speaking."

"Hi, Madison, It's Julienne Taylor. I just got your email."

"Oh! It's great to hear from you. Have you considered the offer?"

"I have," Julienne said. "I would like to accept. When would you like me to start?"

"That's great news," Madison said. "As soon as possible, really. Are you available this week?"

Julienne swallowed. "It's already Wednesday," she said. She had to figure out how to tell Cece, how to extricate herself from Cece's life.

"We really just need someone on the phone," Madison said. "It's really important for our customers."

"I could start Friday," Julienne said.

"Sounds perfect," Madison said. "I'll have someone send over the paperwork."

"Great," Julienne said, feeling inane.

"See you then," Madison said, and hung up.

Julienne swallowed. Hearing Madison's voice had brought back the memory of the last rejection, of hearing that she didn't stand out. And then Cece had said she was uptight, boring.

She *felt* boring. Even though she'd impulsively taken two jobs, even though she was starting to get used to taking chances. It felt like everyone around her was more confident, more willing to take risks.

Carter Gallery were taking a risk on her. She just had to prove she was worth it.

This was her chance to work in a real art gallery, and she was committed to it now.

Who knew how long the gig with Cece would have lasted, anyway. How long would Cece need a minder, how long could their relationship last under that kind of pres-

192 MAX LOUISE PERRY

sure? Working together didn't make sense in the long-term, not with all they'd been through in such a short time.

It was better to get out now.

Figuring out how to tell Cece was her next problem.

She wasn't sure Cece would forgive her for abandoning her, but Sadie had said it was a trial period, and the paparazzi had scared Julienne enough to make her want to run away anyway. That was how she justified it to herself.

She tried not to linger on her hurt feelings from the argument last night, but they were there, and they made her hate herself. She was too weak to be around someone like Cece, who said exactly what she was thinking, all of the time. It was better if she just left.

She typed a query into Google: How to quit a job I've only had for a week?

She wasn't the only person who'd got a better offer after starting a job. She settled in to read the stories of what others had done, and just like always, research calmed her nerves. It made it seem like this was less impulsive, like quitting a job abruptly just happened sometimes.

She could almost forget about Cece.

Almost.

She copied and pasted a draft resignation someone had posted online into an email to Sadie. She edited it, adding a more personal comment about her concerns for her privacy, and wished Cece the best. She saved it as a draft and got up and walked away from her laptop. She did another lap of the apartment, trying to work up the courage to send it.

God, she needed to think. She needed to talk this through with someone, preferably over a drink, but the non-disclosure agreement still hung over her and Sadie's words about staying at home still rung in her ears.

All she had to do to feel less trapped was press send.

She hoped Cece would forgive her, one day, for this.

She changed her mind about not going for a run and got changed, needing to do something to occupy herself.

She thought fresh air and the pounding beats of her music might give her the clarity she needed.

It felt good to sweat, to stop thinking, to focus only on her body. It reminded her a bit of tennis keeping her on an even keel throughout college, even during that awful semester where she got her heart broken and she was so homesick.

She ran for an hour and then walked the last half-mile home. She messaged the group chat and suggested they find somewhere to play tennis at the weekend, wanting a distraction from everything. She was pleased when her phone chimed with her friends agreeing.

Her friends had her back. She didn't need Cece.

When she got home, she went straight to her computer and sent that email draft.

It was too late to go back now.

TWENTY-FOUR

By the next morning, she had three missed calls from Cece and two texts she was afraid to read.

She went to the gym instead of replying, put her phone on silent so even the vibration wouldn't distract her.

She wished she could confide in Tori. She did tell her she quit, though, and Tori asked a lot of questions that Julienne couldn't answer. The non-disclosure agreement felt more and more like it was choking her, but she owed it to Cece to protect her privacy.

She owed Cece more than that, probably, but she tried not to think about it too much.

It was hard not to think about. She tried to focus on her workout, but she could taste guilt on the back of her tongue and all her usual pump-her-up songs weren't working. She swiped through her phone trying to find something different, a new playlist or a podcast or something to take her mind off of it.

What if she'd made a terrible mistake?

Her phone was knocked out of her hand with a slap and

she jumped back, the treadmill coming to a sharp stop as the safety pulled.

"Your phone *is* working, then," Cece said. Her mouth curled in a snarl, and Julienne's insides plummeted to the floor.

Cece's cheeks were flushed red with anger and tears were shining in her eyes and Julienne felt like the worst person in the world.

"You were just gonna ghost me?" Cece demanded. "I don't even get a phone call?"

Julienne's mouth went dry and her mind blank. "Sorry," she managed, her tone wavering.

"Tell me how you really feel, Julienne," Cece said sarcastically. "Would it kill you to actually explain yourself? For once?"

"I'm sorry," Julienne said, more firmly. "I got a job offer I couldn't pass up."

Cece rolled her eyes. People were starting to look over at the two of them, at the fuss Cece was making. Julienne bent to pick up her phone.

"Were you just using me?" Cece said, her voice heart-breakingly soft. "Was all of it fake? Every time you acted like you gave a shit?"

Julienne opened her mouth, but couldn't conjure up a defense. She closed it again. Her face felt hot with shame.

"You really have nothing to say," Cece said. "I can't believe I actually thought you cared about me."

Shame crept from her red cheeks to the back of her neck and inched down her spine. "I do," she said, softly.

"Could've fooled me," Cece spat. "Fuck you, Julienne. I wish I'd never met you."

People were still looking at her as Cece stormed away. For a moment, Julienne froze, as if all of Cece's anger was rooting her to the spot. It took a few breaths before she felt she could move.

She picked up her phone from the floor and went to the changing room, not making eye contact with anyone else. Her heart was still pounding as she emptied her locker and headed straight home.

What had she done?

TWENTY-FIVE

She wanted to crawl into bed and hide from the world. She wanted to show up at Cece's door and beg for forgiveness.

She did neither of those things. It felt like she was running on autopilot as she turned the water temperature all the way up and got in the shower. It hurt a little, to stand there, but she stayed until her skin was all red and she felt like she wouldn't fall apart anymore.

Tori was home by the time she got out of the shower, and Julienne didn't know if she could face her.

She didn't know if she could find the words to explain herself.

She missed Cece, suddenly. She missed the way Cece could smooth out Julienne's edges, the way she made Julienne feel so understood.

It felt like a rug had been pulled out from under her, but she only had herself to blame.

"You okay, J?" Tori asked, knocking gently on the bathroom door.

"I'll be out in a sec," she called out. She threw on some clothes and opened the door.

Tori raised an eyebrow. "You sure you're okay?"

Julienne wondered what she looked like. "Got a new job," she mumbled.

"And you look like you're about to burst into tears because...?"

Julienne shook her head, willing her eyes to dry up. "I don't want to talk about it."

Tori looked worried. "Did you get fired?"

Julienne shook her head again. "I think I'm going to get an early night, okay?"

She could feel Tori watching her as she walked to her bedroom and tried not to feel like the walls were closing in on her.

She'd done this. She'd done this to Cece, and all that was left was for her to stew in her own mistakes.

Once she started the new job, it would all feel worth it, she told herself.

It wasn't very convincing, and she couldn't stop seeing all the hurt on Cece's face.

She curled under the covers and wished she'd never signed that non-disclosure agreement. She wanted to tell someone, anyone. She wanted to get all of her guilt out of her guts and into the open air.

There was a soft knock on the door.

"Yeah?" Julienne called out.

Tori opened the door. "Mia texted me an article about you and Cece," she said. "Also, it's like, 5pm. You're not going to bed yet."

"Oh, god, no wonder she agreed to tennis this weekend," Julienne said, groaning.

"I'm worried about you," Tori said softly.

"I signed an NDA, Tor, I can't talk about it."

"Does that mean it's true?"

Julienne shrugged. She shuffled up her bed to lean against the headboard, and Tori came in and sat on the end of it. "Whatever they're saying probably isn't true. We were in Vegas for work."

It had become more than work so quickly, though.

Her heart felt heavy.

"Tell me about the new job," Tori said, switching gears.

"It's that art gallery I told you about," Julienne said. "It's not the position I interviewed for, but someone left really suddenly, I guess, and they still had my résumé."

"That's awesome, though," Tori said. "Congrats."

Julienne hummed. It didn't feel awesome anymore.

"Are you going to keep in touch with Cece?" Tori asked, gently.

Julienne bit her lip. "I don't think so," she said.

She didn't think that was an option, somehow.

"I might have ghosted her," she admitted.

Tori picked up a pillow and hit her with it. "How many times have you consoled me through being ghosted? You know it's a dick move."

"She said I was uptight!" Julienne said. "We're too different, and it just made sense to take this other job."

"Did you care about each other?" Tori asked.

Julienne shifted uncomfortably in her bed. "I don't know if I'm allowed to answer that."

Tori sighed. "Come on, Julienne, you know how much it hurts to be ghosted."

Julienne looked down at her hands. "I do know," she said. "It was a shitty thing to do."

"I hope this new job is worth it," Tori said.

Julienne bit her lip. "Me too," she said.

It had to be.

"Have you eaten? We could get break up pizza," Tori said.

Julienne pulled a face. "It's not a break up," she said.

She remembered the tears in Cece's eyes.

Maybe it was a little bit of a break up.

She let Tori order pizza regardless, and half an hour later, with grease dripping on her chin in front of an action comedy Tori had picked for its leading actress, she felt a little better.

She put Cece to the back of her mind and tried to focus on her new job. It was all happening so quickly, and she had a list of things she needed to do before she started the following morning. Planning soothed her, making lists and setting aside time to complete them. It kept her mind off Cece, too.

She spent the evening ironing the clothes she planned to wear the next day, trying to remember what people were wearing at the interview so she'd fit in. It hadn't been long, but it felt like she'd been a completely different person when she'd interviewed. So much had happened in such a short time.

She deleted Cece's texts from her phone without looking at them, and ignored the messages from Reina and Mia about the photos they'd seen. She wondered if she'd ever be brave enough to show her face at the gym again.

She planned her route to work, laid out her outfit and set a series of alarms. There was nothing to do but sleep, but she lay awake in bed, anxiety kneading at her gut.

Tomorrow, she'd be working in an art gallery. Tomorrow, she had a second chance.

That thought set her tossing and turning for another hour, till eventually she fell asleep.

She woke before her alarm, dressed exactly as she planned, and ate a healthy, balanced breakfast. She wanted today to go perfectly. She wanted to control every possible factor.

Who cared if that made her uptight? It got the job done.

She tried to remember if she'd been this nervous before she met Cece.

It was easier not to think about it.

She was ready to go far too early, and resisted the urge to anxiously pace. She made idle, nervous conversation with Tori while Tori ate her breakfast.

She just wanted to go, be on the road, move on with her life. If she could just put all her worries about unemployment and all her feelings for Cece in a box that she never had to open again, she would be fine. This job, this miracle that had appeared in her inbox, was the key to doing that.

Worse than the nerves was the tiny flutter of hope in her chest.

On the drive downtown she hit rush hour traffic, and she was glad, at least, she'd set aside some extra time for her journey. Then she couldn't find anywhere to park, and ended up feeding dollar bills into a meter three blocks away from the gallery and power walking in the heat.

She arrived slightly sweaty and only just on time. Madison met her at reception and introduced her to a few people, reeling off names so fast Julienne missed nearly all of them, and then showed her to the back room where she'd be spending the morning. It was a small office, the walls plain white and window bare. For a moment, it reminded Julienne of Cece's place before they'd painted the walls.

"Here's a script, most people call with fairly simple questions," Madison said. "Once you've got the hang of the phone system, we can move you to the front desk and you can take calls from there."

Julienne nodded, looking at the bare desk and the old computer set-up.

The job description had sounded more... involved. She thought she'd actually get to speak to visitors to the art gallery, maybe even about the art on the walls, or she'd get to organise events and tours.

She hadn't even really got to see the art as she was shown around.

She sat on the chair and Madison left her to it. She hadn't even managed to ask her about the parking situation.

The room was a little too warm, and the computer was slow to start up. She typed out the generic password Madison had written down for her and got to work.

The phone started ringing, and she picked it up, following the script to provide directions to the gallery. She tried to remember her chirpy phone manner from the last time she'd worked in customer service, but it was hard to find it in this blank slate of a room where she'd been abandoned. She wished she was at the front desk already. She didn't even know why they had this room tucked away in the back, dedicated to questions that could easily be answered by looking on their website.

She couldn't help but wonder why they'd needed this role filled so urgently.

MAYBE IT WOULD GET BETTER. It was only the first day, after all.

Hours passed, and she quickly picked up the rhythm of the caller's questions. After her lunch break, she sat at the front desk, answering the phones and listening as Deya sold brochures and gave visitors directions. At least from here she could see the art.

About an hour before she was due to finish, Madison checked in with her, asking her if she found everything was okay.

"Is there any room for development in the role?" Julienne asked, realising it was the sort of question you were meant to ask before you're hired.

"Slow down," Madison said, "it's only your first day. We'll talk about it after your first month, if you do well here."

Julienne nodded, wondering why that didn't give her the relief it should. It was everything she wanted, a foot in the door at a career in an art gallery.

She couldn't help but think of Cece.

Madison interrupted her thoughts, stopping them from getting too far: "By the way, can you come in tomorrow?"

Julienne swallowed. "I have plans."

Madison's brow creased. "I'd really appreciate it. It's busier on the weekend, so there would be more for you to do."

Julienne could feel her resolve weakening. She needed this job, after all.

"I could do the morning," she said.

"Great," Madison said. "I won't be here, but just introduce yourself to whoever's on the front desk and they'll set you up."

Madison left without saying goodbye, leaving Julienne blinking after her.

When it got to 6pm, Deya showed her how to shut the system down, and then she left. She felt strangely lonely, for a day spent meeting new people.

The thought bugged her, tickling at the back of her brain as she drove home.

This was everything she wanted. It was the opportunity she'd desperately needed, and it had fallen into her lap.

So why wasn't she happy?

TWENTY-SIX

Madison was right, the gallery was busier on the weekend. She met more of the team, and talked to more of the customers in person. It helped that one of her favourite art pieces was on the path between the front desk and the staff toilet, but even getting the chance to look at it a few times a day didn't help to quell the strange empty feeling inside her. Nobody seemed to begrudge her leaving early – in fact, everyone she'd met at the gallery so far had been nice. It almost made her forget that Madison had said she didn't stand out.

She wondered who got the job she had interviewed for the first time.

It was weird putting on her tennis dress again. It had been months since they'd played, mostly because Reina was the instigator of the group. It was strange to meet without her, really, but the four of them made for a better game anyway.

She bounced a tennis ball a few times and served, watched as it went whistling by Aubrey's head.

"I'm a little hungover," Aubrey called out.

Julienne laughed.

It had been years since she'd played for fun, rather than training or competition. The rhythm of the tennis ball was soothing, as familiar as her own heartbeat.

They slipped back into the same camaraderie they'd had in college, focusing on the game instead of conversation. They took a water break after the first match, and Mia honed in on Julienne.

"So you and Cece Browne, huh?" she said.

Julienne rolled her eyes. "I signed an NDA," she said.

"Interesting," Mia said, rolling the world around her mouth. "So you *were* dating."

"No," Julienne said. "I can't tell you anything. That's what an NDA means."

Mia sighed wistfully. "Love, undisclosed," she said. "So romantic."

"Leave it, Mia," Julienne said, a little more firmly.

Mia pouted.

The next match started off a little awkwardly, but that didn't stop Julienne and Mia from winning. They played another match, and then another, before Aubrey finally demanded they give up on tennis and go get some food.

Julienne remembered Sadie's warning to lay low for a few days, but she figured nobody would be looking for her with her friends after a tennis match. It wasn't like she was really famous.

It wasn't like she was Cece.

That was a thought that needed a drink to accompany it, so she ordered wine with her meal at the tapas place Tori had found on her phone.

"How was work this morning?" Tori asked her.

Julienne shrugged. "It was fine, I guess."

Even when she was surrounded by beautiful art, the

kind she would have written essays about in college, she couldn't get Cece out of her head.

Tori frowned at her, but didn't say anything.

Julienne just shrugged.

"I thought you started a new job a few weeks ago?" Aubrey asked.

Julienne glanced at Tori. She should have thought of this, come up with some answers beforehand. "I worked for a publicist for like a week. It didn't work out."

"That's how you met Cece, right?" Mia said, leaning forward and gesturing enthusiastically with her fork.

"It was a work thing, yeah," Julienne said cautiously.

Mia grinned. "And then it became more."

"Stop writing fanfiction about them in your head, you weirdo," Tori said.

Mia laughed. "I just want to know about your brush with fame!"

Cece had done more than just brush against her, and Julienne felt her cheeks warm up at the memory of Cece's bare skin against hers.

"She's blushing," Aubrey said.

Julienne rolled her eyes. "I'm legally not allowed to talk about it."

"I bet it was fun, though, right? Cece seems like she'd be a lot of fun."

"Mia, jesus," Julienne said.

Mia lifted her hands in apology. She did look a little pleased she'd finally got a reaction out of Julienne, though.

Tori gave Julienne a sympathetic look. "How's your love life, Mia?" she said pointedly.

Aubrey laughed. "What love life?"

"Hey!"

After that, they relaxed into easy chatter, Aubrey telling

them about the adventurous date they had planned for the next day.

Julienne wondered what it would be like for Cece to be a part of this conversation. Cece had only mentioned wanting to meet Reina, but Julienne wondered if Cece would fit in with this group.

Or would she just realise that Julienne wasn't anyone interesting, after all.

They lingered over the meal, none of them eager to end the evening, and then Tori drove Julienne back to their apartment.

"Thanks for sticking up for me with Mia," Julienne said, as they climbed the stairs to their apartment building.

Tori shrugged. "She should respect people's boundaries more."

"It's just as well me and Cece aren't a thing anymore," Julienne said. "She would not be able to cope."

There was a pause as Tori fumbled for her keys and unlocked the apartment door.

"Are you sure you're okay?" Tori asked. "You sound really sad when you talk about her."

The question froze Julienne in her place, still in the doorway of their dark apartment.

"I didn't know I could miss someone this much," she said quietly. "I hardly even know her."

Tori gave her a small smile. "You know her enough."

Julienne swallowed. Tori flicked the light on and Julienne shook herself, following her inside.

It was too late to miss Cece. She couldn't undo what she'd done. She hadn't been brave enough to tell Cece what was actually going on, and she deserved Cece's anger for that.

"Maybe it would be easier if I just moved back to England," she said, thinking aloud.

"No way," Tori said. She opened the fridge and started rummaging through it. "You love LA. This is your home. You can't run away just because of a girl."

"You just don't want to find another roommate," Julienne said, as Tori grabbed a half empty bottle of white wine from the fridge.

"Want some?" she asked. Julienne nodded. Tori carried on: "I like living with you. We've got each other's backs."

She filled a glass and passed it to Julienne. It was easy to forget that they hadn't always been this close. They'd met as college freshmen, awkwardly lingering around the edges of an event put on for LGBT student athletes.

They'd come a long way since then. She curled up on the sofa, one arm around a rainbow cushion.

"I did miss you, when you worked with Cece," Tori said. "I have to bounce article ideas off a rubber duck, now."

Julienne snorted.

"Tell me, were all those overnights work or pleasure?"

"Shut up," Julienne said. She took a sip. "We went to Vegas for work and our flight got cancelled so we had to stay overnight."

"That wasn't the only time," Tori said.

Julienne rolled her eyes. "It was all work," she said. "And I still signed an NDA."

"Roommate privileges," Tori said.

Julienne laughed. "You're a journalist, you should know better."

Tori grimaced. "I don't feel like a journalist. Not a real one, anyways."

"Of course you're a real journalist!" Julienne exclaimed. "How's the networking going?"

"Better, I think. There's talk of starting up a mentoring program, I thought I might sign up to be a mentee."

Julienne nodded encouragingly.

Tori sighed. "I just want my boss to actually like my writing."

"I'm sure they do," Julienne said.

Tori shook her head. "Ugh, I don't want to talk about work." She took a long swig of her wine, then refilled her glass.

"I should love my job," Julienne said. "I don't know why I don't."

Tori sighed. "This graduate thing isn't all it's cracked up to be, is it?"

Julienne hummed in agreement, tipping her head back to look up at the ceiling.

"I don't know what I want any more," she said. It was the first time she'd said it out loud.

Tori sighed. "I miss college. When we had dreams that weren't affected by reality."

Julienne laughed.

"Jesus, this wine is really hitting me," Tori said. "I should go to bed."

She rose from her chair, passing Julienne the nearly empty wine bottle to finish.

"Goodnight," Julienne said.

Tori pointed at her. "Don't stay up too late being sad," she said.

Julienne laughed. "I'll try not to."

Tori shut her bedroom door and Julienne was left alone, a glass of half-drunk wine in her hand and a brewing headache.

The sadness crept in quicker when she was alone. Her phone buzzed with a text from Sadie.

Sadie: I don't know what you and Cece talked about, but it must have gotten through to her! Production says her attitude has been way better this week. Hope she keeps it up! If not, may have to steal you back :)

Maybe Cece didn't need her anymore. Maybe it was just Julienne feeling the empty space where Cece had been.

She missed the way Cece filled up a whole room, captured her whole attention. Her bright smile seemed to blot out any bad mood.

She'd never met anyone like Cece before.

She wasn't sure she ever would again.

TWENTY-SEVEN

Her head was only slightly sluggish in the morning, but she still decided to punish herself by going back to the gym. The term she'd pre-paid months ago was coming to an end, and she was going to cancel her membership soon anyway. She had to make the most of it till then.

She planned ahead and wore her gym clothes, not wanting to linger in the changing room in case anyone who'd been witness to her very public argument with Cece showed up.

It wasn't busy when she got there, still a little early for the Sunday morning crowd. She didn't make eye contact with anyone, just tried to focus on getting through her workout. Her muscles ached a little from tennis the previous day, but it was an ache that felt familiar. It made her feel strong.

She was sweating hard by the time she finished her workout and moved on to the cool down. She noticed someone giving her an odd look, and she thought she heard Cece's name as she was switching between playlists, but she told herself she was hearing things. It was a weekend, it was just a different crowd than she was used to.

Sweat slid down her spine and her hands were slippery on the buttons of the treadmill. She regretted her decision not to bring a change of clothes, not looking forward to the walk home while she was still hot and sweaty.

There were two teenagers lingering in the gym foyer, and Julienne wondered what it would be like to grow up in LA. She'd spent her early childhood in Southern California, but she had a feeling England was a very different place to spend your teenage years.

The doors swung open with a swish and Julienne braced herself for leaving the air conditioning.

Instead, there was a shout and the click of a camera lens.

For a second, Julienne froze, transported back to that morning in Vegas, crude words shouted at her.

"Why'd Cece Browne dump you?" someone yelled. Julienne blinked at them, feeling sweat trickle down her spine.

"What's your name? Are you a lesbian? Is she? We'll pay for an exclusive."

She turned on her heel and ran back into the gym. The lone photographer tried to follow, but the receptionist was on her feet and telling him to leave.

The teenagers were giggling. One of them had their phone up, filming Julienne.

She was sweating, exposed, still in her gym clothes.

"That's enough, girls," the receptionist said, as one of them moved closer.

There was a peal of laughter, and Julienne hunched her shoulders, trying to make herself smaller.

The receptionist rolled her eyes at them. "Come on," she said. "I'll let you in to the staffroom."

Julienne nodded. "Thanks," she croaked, and followed the receptionist.

"I'm not famous," she said. She didn't know why she said it. She focused on the receptionist's name tag: Molly.

Molly shrugged. "I think one of those girls might have called someone. They were waiting in the lobby for something to happen."

Julienne sighed.

"They won't be allowed back," Molly said. "You can leave out the staff entrance, if you want."

"I walked here," Julienne said. It was hard to form sentences. "I don't want them to know where I live."

"I can call someone for you?"

"Tori," Julienne said. "She'll know what to do."

She pulled out her phone and called Tori. The phone rang and rang and she tried not to worry too much about swearing on the staff room sofa.

It went to voicemail. Julienne swore softly and pressed her forehead to her knees.

'Why'd Cece Browne dump you?' echoed in her head.

The only other person she could think to call was Cece. Cece, who had been here before, who would know what to do.

She passed Molly her phone and asked her to talk to Cece, not willing to do it herself.

Maybe that made her a coward.

"She's on her way," Molly said, after a brief conversation. "She didn't sound happy about it."

Julienne shut her eyes, trying to quell the fear churning in her stomach. At least she was coming, she told herself.

She waited in silence in the staff room, feeling the sweat on her skin grow cold. Molly left her alone, going back to her front desk duties.

Hot shame flushed her neck and she was almost folded in on herself by the time Cece knocked on the back door. Her limbs felt stiff and her movements unnatural as she crossed the room to open the door.

"Hey," Cece said, voice flat and face blank.

"Hi," Julienne said. She sounded as miserable as she felt.

Cece glanced at her phone. "I don't have a lot of time, I have to get back to set. I'll give you a ride home, or wherever."

"Thanks," Julienne said. She followed Cece out to her car, a few paces behind her.

She didn't know what to say.

"You stink, by the way," Cece said, closing the car door with a thunk.

"Sorry," Julienne said. "I called my roommate, but she didn't pick up. I didn't know who else to call."

Cece made a noise in the back of her throat. "They wouldn't be here if it wasn't for me," she said. "That's why I came."

Julienne nodded. Cece threw the car into drive and pulled out, and Julienne swivelled her head to see if anyone was still waiting by the main entrance.

God, she hated this.

The silence was tense. Julienne didn't dare break it to point out that Cece had missed the turn off for her apartment.

"You're not gonna say anything?" Cece said, as they waited in the queues of traffic. "You don't have anything to say to me?"

"I don't know what to say," Julienne said.

"I never lied to you," Cece said. "Why did you even kiss me? Did it mean anything at all to you?"

Julienne swallowed.

"It meant everything," she said quietly.

"Then why did you bail? You could have just talked to me."

Julienne looked at her, but Cece's eyes were on the road, her hands clenched tight around the steering wheel.

"It was easier to run away," Julienne said softly. "I panicked. All those cameras freaked me out."

"You *ghosted* me," Cece said. "Be honest, was it the paparazzi or was it me you were running away from?"

Julienne sighed. This was the hardest conversation she'd ever had.

"Both, maybe," she said.

"Maybe?" Cece said, incredulous. "You don't even know why you did it! Do you know how much that hurt? You just disappeared after I let you in to my life."

"I don't know how to be like you," Julienne said, her voice going pitchy with panic. "I don't know how to be up front, put all my cards on the table. I'm not like that! I'm boring and uptight, remember?"

"I was drunk and I didn't mean it," Cece said, sounding exasperated. "You make everything more difficult than it has to be." She tapped on the steering wheel for emphasis. "Everything."

"I'm sorry," Julienne said, softly. "I didn't know how to do my job when I cared about you so much. I didn't want to let Sadie down."

"Yeah, cause Sadie's feelings are the important ones," Cece said sarcastically as she pulled into the studio parking lot.

"I said I was sorry," Julienne said.

"You really think that's enough?" Cece asked, looking

her in the eyes for the first time. "One apology and all that hurt is gone?"

"I made a mistake," Julienne said.

"Whatever," Cece said, her tone going flat. "You can use the shower in my trailer. Borrow some clean clothes. You can get an Uber or wait a few hours and I'll drive you home, I don't care."

Julienne swallowed. Cece made her feel so small and the worst part was, she deserved it. "Okay," she said. "Thank you."

Cece gave her a curt nod and walked off. Julienne took a second to take a deep breath and gather herself before she got out of the car.

She tried not to think about what she looked like, what people on set might be thinking of her, and headed straight for Cece's trailer. She tried not to think at all, but Cece's words still stung, all the truth in them working its way under her skin and sticking there.

Cece had shown Julienne all of her worst parts without even thinking about it. Julienne couldn't even face the reality of her own feelings.

The trailer was quiet, and Julienne could almost forget she was on Cece's set on a Sunday afternoon. Cece's bathroom was small, the shower almost jutting over the toilet, and Julienne only allowed herself a few minutes under the spray.

She wished Tori had picked up the phone. She wished she'd thought to call someone else, instead. She wished she'd never ghosted Cece. All the different paths they could have gone down cycled through her head, an endless parade of her mistakes.

She wrapped herself in a towel and tried not to feel strange as she looked through Cece's drawers to find some clothes. It felt like an invasion of privacy even though Cece had given her permission. She picked out a plain tank top and a pair of denim shorts, hoping they were generic enough that they wouldn't be missed.

The knowledge that she'd have to see Cece again to return these clothes sat like a rock on her chest. She'd ghosted her to get away from the uncomfortable truth of their situation, and yet still she couldn't seem to extricate herself.

The worst part was, she wanted to see her again. She wanted to get on her knees and beg for forgiveness, tell her that her life was dimmer without Cece in it.

Her phone buzzed with a notification. One of the teenagers from the gym had tagged her in a photo. She untagged herself and hit the report icon, but she didn't know if it would do anything.

The only person who would understand was Cece.

Guilt rendered her inert on the sofa. Her hair hung around her shoulders, still wet from the shower. She had to do something, but she didn't know what.

She tried calling Tori again. No answer. She texted the group chat to see if anyone was free, but nobody responded.

She could just get a cab and get out of there, but the thought that if she did that, she might never see Cece again held her back.

She didn't want to go into work at her very ordinary job at the art gallery tomorrow without at least trying to keep Cece in her life. She'd dreamed of living in LA forever and now LA without Cece seemed empty and dull, like the shine had been rubbed off.

She tugged on her sneakers and folded her clothes so she could grab them later, and then she shut the door to the trailer behind her and crossed over to the studio building.

Set was busy, people Julienne didn't recognise walking around with some haste. They weren't filming yet, and it took a moment for Julienne to spot Cece, sitting in a chair with her name on it, thumbing through a script.

She swallowed.

She didn't know what she was going to say yet. She was winging it, something she'd never learned how to do.

As she got closer, she could see the expression on Cece's face was stormy as her lips mouthed words from the script.

"Cece," Julienne said, interrupting her.

Cece looked up and scowled at her. "I'm working," she said. "I don't have time for this."

Julienne took a deep breath, trying to force the words out. "I need to apologise."

Cece checked the time on her phone. "Do you?"

Julienne swallowed and nodded. "Everything seemed to be going wrong, and then I got another job offer, a job I thought I wanted, and it was so easy to just say yes and pretend that meant everything went away. I thought I could forget you. I thought it would be easier for both of us if I just disappeared."

Cece just sat there, waiting.

"I'm so sorry," Julienne said.

Cece tapped her fingers against the script. "Why should I believe you?" she said.

Julienne opened her mouth, then closed it again.

"I don't know," she said. "I wish I had the answer."

"You just want to be nice, all the damn time," Cece said. "I thought I could trust you. I thought you understood me."

"I do," Julienne said. "I-"

Cece cut her off. "I don't want to hear it. Figure your shit out, Jules. I am not screwing up this job for you."

Julienne closed her mouth with a click. Cece put her

script aside and stood up, taking a moment to put her game face on.

Julienne watched her walk away, her mouth dry and heart aching.

She'd tried. She'd had her chance with Cece, and she'd screwed it up.

She still wanted to win her back, but she needed a plan. She needed to follow her heart, but she needed to figure out how, first.

TWENTY-EIGHT

"So..." Tori said, as Julienne got in her car. "How did you end up here, exactly?"

"Well, if you had answered your phone the first time I called," Julienne said. "I wouldn't have been here at all."

"I was on the phone with my dad," Tori said. "Seriously, what happened?"

Julienne sighed. "Some teenagers at the gym called TMZ or something. I freaked out. I ended up calling Cece to come get me."

"Are you wearing her clothes right now?"

"I didn't bring a change."

"I know you're not allowed to tell me," Tori said. "but I have to say it out loud just in case: did you and Cece just hook up?"

"Not even close," Julienne said. "I don't think she ever wants to see me again."

"You okay?"

Julienne nodded, her jaw set. "I am going to win her back," she said.

She looked over at Tori. She was smiling.

"What?" Julienne asked.

"I've never heard you do your tennis voice about a girl," Tori said. "All determined to win."

Julienne laughed. "I've never met anyone like her before, T."

"Are you going to stand outside her window with a boombox?"

Julienne pulled a face. "There has to be something better than that."

"What would she want you to do?" Tori asked.

"I don't know," Julienne said, as Tori parked her car. "She said she can't trust me. I don't know how to prove that she can."

They climbed the stairs in silence, Julienne considering her options. She wanted to prove to Cece, and maybe to herself, that she understood her.

She thought back to the times when Cece had been most open with her, the times when she'd felt like they understood each other. The date in the bookstore and the conversations they'd had while repainting her house sprung to mind. It was strange to think they'd only spent about a week together, total, though it seemed like their conversations had covered so much of their lives.

She wanted to do something that would make Cece's world brighter; something that would get her back for all the good things she'd given Julienne. Just one week together had been more of an adventure than the rest of Julienne's life, and she didn't want to let that go.

Maybe it was wearing Cece's clothes that made her want to do something rash and impulsive, like her personality rubbed off on them. She wanted to announce from the rooftops that she needed Cece in her life, make a public statement to TMZ or some other awful publication, begging for Cece to come back.

She didn't think Cece would want that.

Tori left her to her thinking, saying she was going to veg out for the rest of the afternoon, and Julienne changed out of Cece's clothes. It felt strange to keep wearing them around the apartment, especially when she was turning her time with Cece over and over in her head, looking for a way she could prove to Cece that she understood her.

She had so much to prove.

She called her mum, instead, a college-favorite way of procrastinating, and told her about her new job. Her mum was thrilled, and pleased too that Julienne wasn't avoiding talking to her anymore, and then she asked for Julienne's work address to send some flowers.

It was a lovely thought, that even an art gallery could be improved by a touch of love from her mother. She didn't have many reminders of her family in the US; in all the years she'd been over here she'd never bothered to put up photos. Suddenly, with a jolt of inspiration, she knew what she had to do for Cece.

She told her mum she loved her and hung up. Immediately, she switched to research mode. She wanted to share the warmth from her mum with Cece, and she knew that like her, Cece didn't have a lot of reminders of her family in her life.

Julienne could fix that.

She remembered Cece mentioning, in one of those early, oddly-intimate conversations, that she'd gotten rid of a lot of things that reminded her of her mother a few years ago. Julienne was determined to get them back. She wondered if she could help with Cece's other problem, about not being ready to come out, but she didn't want to pressure her into anything.

She started on social media, trying not to be intimidated by wading into the social media conversation about Cece. It was filled with speculation about their relationship, which was uncomfortable to read. She didn't want to know what all the fan accounts thought about Cece's sexuality, or whether Julienne was paid to hang out with her, or any other rumours they could come up with. She focused on the fan accounts, scrolling back through the timeline, trying to figure out if any of them had seen the eBay sale. She didn't even know what year it was, which made it harder to find, and she wasn't an expert at searching social media.

She kept scrolling till late in the night, finding it hard to stop and put her phone down once the idea was in her head. Tori would know how to find it, if it was even possible, but Julienne wasn't about to wake her up for this.

She gave up in the early hours of the morning and fell asleep.

It took a lot of effort the next morning to put her game face on for the art gallery. She kept getting distracted by the thought of Cece, fumbling her words when talking to customers about a piece of art she could describe in her sleep. When the desk was quiet, she did more research on her phone, seeing if she could find Cece's eBay account or if Cece herself had ever announced the eBay sale.

Her shift dawdled by, minutes slowly becoming hours. She waved goodbye to Deya but didn't stop to talk to her as she left. She hoped Tori would be home when she got there, but the apartment was empty, so she set up her laptop on the couch and opened all the tabs she thought she would need.

She tried not to feel weird about how much of Cece's

life was documented, posted online, and reacted to by fans. It felt like a strange violation to read this; a fan conversation she shouldn't be a part of.

Tori arriving home interrupted her just as she was starting to have doubts about her plan.

"Hey," Tori said. "You alright?"

"I figured out what I need to do," Julienne said. "But I need your help."

Tori grinned. "This sounds fun, what's up?"

"How do you search someone's social media for a specific word?"

Tori's smile dropped. "You're not like, stalking-stalking Cece, are you?"

"It's not like that, I'm trying to get her a gift," Julienne said, and explained the situation.

Tori nodded slowly. "Let me get changed and then I'll show you. It's pretty easy."

It wasn't long before Tori returned, now wearing sweatpants. She demonstrated how to do the search on Julienne's computer, and then went to the kitchen to cook dinner.

It didn't take long before Julienne found a tweet from Cece announcing the eBay sale with a few promising replies, but none of those led to anything concrete.

"Tori?" she called out. "Can you search for a specific time period?"

"Just a sec," Tori said. There was the sound of something sizzling in a frying pan, and a pause. "Can you bring your laptop over here?"

Julienne moved her laptop to the kitchen counter and watched as Tori skillfully tossed garlic and shallots in a pan.

"When do you want?" Tori asked.

Julienne gave the date of Cece's announcement, and thought maybe a month after might do. She didn't really know what she was looking for, but she had a feeling she'd know it when she saw it.

She scrolled through the search, looking for tweets that mentioned Cece. There were a few fan accounts who seemed excited to have bought things, but none of them mentioned anything other than clothing. She did laugh at the photos posted of a much younger Cece wearing some of the clothes on the Disney show she'd briefly starred in.

"I'm not getting anywhere," she told Tori.

"Maybe check Instagram?" Tori said. "Or you could reach out to a fan account, see if they would help."

"Some fan accounts are already talking about me," Julienne said. "I don't want to add any fuel to that fire. Plus there's still the NDA."

"Try different words and phrases," Tori said. "Sorry, my brain is kind of fried. It has been a *day*."

Julienne made a sympathetic noise, and Tori returned her focus to her food. Julienne listened as she vented about some shit her boss had pulled, and made noises in all the right places. Eventually, Tori's dinner was done, and she sat down opposite Julienne to eat. Julienne kept searching, not bothering to think about what she might eat. She needed to at some point, but this was more important.

She kept scrolling through Twitter, trying different versions of 'award', 'trophy', and Cece's name.

She almost dropped her phone when she saw it.

Wren @addictedtostanning Apr 10 2017

omg the trophy I bought from Cece's eBay arrived!! it's her first im so hyyype

Julienne bookmarked the tweet and clicked through to the person's profile, praying they were still active on Twitter. Their last tweet was earlier that day, and their DMs were open. Julienne tried not to think too much as she typed out a message.

Julienne @Jnotanartist: Hi! I have kind of a weird request, I'm looking for an old award of Cece Browne's and I'm pretty sure you bought one a few years ago... do you still have it? I can buy it off you. You'd be doing me a huge favor!

Wren @addictedtostanning: ur right that is weird :p i do still have it, are u a collector or what?

Julienne put her phone down, taking a second to think about her reply.

Julienne @Jnotanartist: I'd prefer not to say if that's okay?

Wren @addictedtostanning: i don't really want to give it to a random

Shit. Julienne took a deep breath and then chose her words very carefully.

Julienne @Jnotanartist: I actually know Cece irl and she mentioned she regretted selling it. I thought it would be a nice surprise

Wren started typing, and then stopped.

Julienne put her phone face down, unwilling to stare at the screen. The waiting was killing her.

"You okay?" Tori asked, close to finishing her plate of food.

"I think I found it," Julienne said. "I just need to convince this person to give it to me."

Tori raised her eyebrows. Julienne's phone vibrated loudly on the counter and they both looked at it.

Julienne turned it over.

Wren @addictedtostanning: can u prove u know her?

Julienne sighed.

"They want me to prove I know Cece," she said.

"Just send her a photo of yourself," Tori said. "Aren't there photos of you together already?"

"I feel like I need a lawyer for this conversation," Julienne said, burying her head in her hands.

Tori shrugged, moving her plate over to the side of the sink. "It's not like they suddenly own all photos of you, right?"

Julienne nodded. "But I don't want to draw any more attention to Cece. Or to me."

"Or get sued," Tori added, helpfully.

A pang of anxiety stirred in her gut.

Cece had deleted the photo of them together from her Instagram, so Julienne couldn't even use that. She went back through her messages from Mia, wondering if one of the articles Mia had sent her might have something she could use.

She found it in the group chat, in the messages she'd ignored because she was too shaken up: a screenshot of the photo of her and Cece together.

It hurt a little to look at, to remember how comfortable Cece had been that first night, telling Julienne she looked hot and perching on her arm.

She missed it.

She sent it to Wren and waited.

Wren @addictedtostanning: wait r u the person that was in vegas with Cece!!! are u dating??

She tried to find a way to word the truth that wouldn't violate the NDA. She didn't want to manipulate Wren, either.

Julienne @Jnotanartist: we are friends :) just wanted to do something nice for her bc of all the press. you'd really be helping me out

Wren @addictedtostanning: alright, i'm in! where do u want me to send it?

Julienne @Jnotanartist: oh my god, thank you so much! How much do you want for it?

She typed out her address and sent it.

Wren @addictedtostanning: can u pay for shipping? i can send u a receipt :) i would love a pic of Cece holding it tho? Or maybe like a video of her sayin thank u? idk whatever works!

Julienne @Jnotanartist: I can't promise anything, bc I want it to be a surprise, but I'll see what I can do!

Wren @addictedtostanning: i'll send it tomorrow!!

Julienne exhaled. That was it. It was happening.

She had a good feeling about this.

TWENTY-NINE

Julienne spent the next few days anxiously waiting for the trophy to arrive. Wren had sent her a receipt and she'd sent them money, so she knew, or hoped, that it was on its way.

She missed Cece. She felt her absence every day she went to the gallery, every day that passed by without a glimmer of excitement. She missed when her life had been unpredictable.

Tori texted her on Thursday that a package had arrived for her, and it took all of Julienne's self restraint not to leave work early and rush home.

She needed this job, she told herself. It felt like she needed Cece a little more, though.

Her shift finally over, she barely said goodbye to Deya and went straight to her car. She was full of nervous energy as she drove home, and the LA traffic was even more frustrating than usual.

She hadn't really thought beyond getting the trophy; she didn't have a plan beyond showing up wherever Cece was.

She should have written a speech, she thought, as she

climbed the stairs to the apartment. She'd had days to prepare, after all. But if Cece had taught her anything, it was that sometimes winging it was the best option.

Tori had left the parcel on the kitchen counter, and Julienne tore it open with a pair of kitchen scissors. Encased in layers of bubble wrap was a golden trophy, Cece Browne and Young Artist Award 2014 delicately engraved in the plaque. It had a hefty weight to it, too, and Julienne was careful not to get any fingermarks on it as she lifted it out of the packaging.

It was here. She was really doing this.

She checked Cece's social media on her phone, just in case her plans for the evening would somehow be available, but she hadn't posted anything in nearly a week. Julienne hoped that wasn't her fault.

It took three drafts to get a text worded in a way she was happy with.

Julienne: Are you free this evening? I wanted to bring your clothes I borrowed back, maybe clear the air?

Cece: yeah whatever

It was about as enthusiastic a response as Julienne deserved. She changed out of her work clothes and put on jeans and a blouse, then grabbed the clothes she'd washed and folded and the trophy. Tori poked her head out of her bedroom door to wish her luck.

There was no turning back now, and if this didn't work – it didn't bear thinking about.

She drummed her fingers on the steering wheel the whole drive over, unable to sit still. She kept glancing over at the trophy, delicately placed on her passenger seat, making sure it was real and still there.

She hoped it would be enough.

She parked outside of Cece's place and took a few deep

breaths. Her exhales were shaky and it felt like her veins were thrumming with energy.

She only had one shot at this.

She'd never taken this kind of risk for someone she cared about before. She didn't even think she'd ever liked someone as much as she liked Cece. Winning Cece back felt like the most important thing she'd ever done. She couldn't imagine her life without Cece in it.

She slid the trophy in the top of the bag she'd filled with Cece's clothes, trying to imagine getting it out and giving it to her. She was thinking too much, planning too much, but her mind kept whirring as she approached Cece's front door and rang the bell.

Cece was slow to answer and when she finally opened the door, the look on her face only increased Julienne's nerves.

"Hey," Cece said, her tone flat.

"Hi," Julienne said.

Her limbs felt stiff and uncooperative. Cece didn't move, either, so they just stood there, looking at each other.

Julienne thought about counting the freckles on Cece's nose.

"Can I come in?" she said, her mouth a little dry.

Cece stepped aside so she could enter. "You could have just mailed them," she said.

"I wanted to see you," Julienne said.

Cece snorted. "Didn't want to wait till you needed another rescue?"

Julienne bit her lip. "I'm sorry. I ran because I was scared of how much I liked you and what that meant."

"You've already apologised," Cece said. "I don't know what you want me to say."

"Can I show you something?"

Cece rolled her eyes.

"Please," Julienne said, her heart in her throat. She didn't know what she'd do if Cece said no.

Cece gestured for her to continue.

"I wish you knew how much I cared about you," Julienne blurted out. Then, a little slower: "We haven't known each other that long, but you changed my life. I should have trusted in that. I should have trusted you, and I should have been someone you could trust."

Cece's face had softened a little, the scowl on her brow fading.

"I wanted to get you something," Julienne said. "Something to prove that I understand you and I care about you and I want to be in your life."

"What are you talking about?" Cece said.

Julienne took a long, shaky breath. She reached into her bag and pulled out the award. "This is yours."

Cece's eyes widened. "But this is... is this the original? My first award? How did you find this?"

"It's the original," Julienne confirmed. "I did some digging on social media. My roommate helped."

Cece's eyes were filling with tears and Julienne wanted to step closer and crush her into a hug.

She didn't know if Cece wanted that.

"Thank you," Cece said, her voice a little hoarse. "Nobody's ever done something like that for me before."

"I don't want you to think trusting me was a mistake," Julienne said.

Julienne watched as Cece took the trophy from her and ran a thumb over the engraving on its base. She had to blink a little hard, at that.

"My first ever award ceremony," Cece said. Her damp eyes began leaking, leaving tear-tracks down her cheeks.

"We already knew mom was dying. She was so proud of me, she didn't care about anyone else there. She gave a really embarrassing interview."

Julienne still felt stiff, standing at the threshold, unsure if Cece wanted her or not.

"Can I give you a hug?" she said, her voice soft.

Cece nodded, her eyes still on the trophy.

Moments ago, the space between them had seemed vast, but Julienne crossed it in two paces and pressed Cece to her chest.

"I was thinking," she said. "I don't want to pressure you to do anything. But maybe you could write your mom a letter, coming out to her. Keep it with the trophy. It sounded like it was important to you."

Cece rested her head against Julienne's shoulder and sniffed. Her arms were so tight around Julienne it almost hurt, but Julienne didn't want to let go. They stood like that in silence, the door still open behind them, for a few long moments.

Cece lifted her head. "I think that's a really good idea," she said. "Thank you, it means a lot."

Julienne tilted her head to look Cece in the eyes. "I know I was a shitty person, but I am going to make it up to you."

The ghost of a smile crossed Cece's lips. "You already have," she said. Her eyes flicked down to Julienne's lips, and Julienne swallowed.

"Can I–" she was cut off by the press of Cece's lips against her own, swallowing her words.

Their noses, teeth, lips, tongues brushed against each other, clumsy and needy and gentle all at once. Cece's face was still damp with tears, the sharp edges of the trophy pressing into Julienne's back.

Julienne gasped for air when they parted, the taste of Cece's lipbalm still on her lips.

"I love you," she blurted out, without thinking about it.

Cece's mouth slowly curved into a smile. "Yeah, okay," she said. She stepped back and Julienne missed the weight of her immediately, but she just reached out an arm to flick the front door closed, and then pulled Julienne further in to her condo.

"You're so confusing," Cece told her, but she sounded delighted by it.

Julienne couldn't resist, she pressed another kiss to the corner of Cece's smile. "I try," she said.

Cece laughed.

Julienne wished she could freeze the world for a moment, take a snapshot of Cece's laugh, head tossed back, eyes gleaming. Julienne could lose herself in those brown eyes.

Instead, Cece pressed in close again and they kissed, a little less clumsy than before. The heat of Cece's lips, of Cece's body, went straight to Julienne's head. She wasn't sure she'd ever recover from it. Cece crowded her backwards and pressed her against the wall, and Julienne felt the heat of her all throughout her body.

It was electrifying.

They seemed to speak in half sentences: "We should–", "Do you want–", broken up by kisses, by the friction of their bodies, by gasps for air.

It was only afterward, when Julienne's heart rate had slowed a little, and the flush on Cece's cheeks had faded, that either of them managed to speak full sentences again.

"Do you want to be my girlfriend?" Cece asked, looking earnest. Then: "Also, do you want a drink?"

Julienne let out a startled laugh. "Yes," she said. "To both, I mean."

Cece grinned at her and Julienne wondered if she would ever get tired of Cece's smile.

She put the trophy on an empty shelf, in pride of place, and they both paused for a second to admire it.

"I'm going to text Sadie that we can start talking about coming out," Cece said. "I think I might be ready."

"She's going to kill me," Julienne said.

Cece's smile just got wider, showing her gums. "She'll get over it," she said, her phone already in one hand, typing.

"You're amazing," Julienne said, then put her hand over her mouth. She hadn't meant to say that out loud.

Cece's cheeks turned pink. "I'm just doing what makes me happy," she said.

"I wish I was that brave," Julienne said.

Cece looked her in the eye. "You're here, aren't you?"

EPILOGUE

The cameras flashed, and Cece's arm was a comforting weight around her waist.

"You okay?" Cece murmured into Julienne's ear.

Julienne nodded, looking at the array of photographers standing opposite as they posed. It was her first red carpet, and there was a knot of anxiety in her stomach that wouldn't ease.

Cece made her feel brave, though, in spite of the cameras.

They changed pose, and then Julienne stepped aside to allow Cece to be photographed on her own, in her beautiful designer suit. Sometimes when she woke up beside Cece, she couldn't believe this was her reality. This glamorous, outrageous woman was such a huge part of her life.

Julienne was wearing a dusky pink midi dress Cece had helped her choose and her hair was styled by someone Sadie had hired, but for all her nerves about fitting in with the star-studded crowd, she didn't really care what she looked like when she was beside Cece.

The night before, she'd called her parents and finally

introduced them to Cece, in video form. They knew of her, they knew bare details, but it was nice to do a formal introduction.

Cece had told them they'd met at the gym. That was what they told everyone who asked. Julienne imagined one day they'd tell the whole story.

Cece gestured for Julienne to rejoin her, photos done with, and they moved further down the red carpet, pausing occasionally for photos. Cece chatted to a few of her co-stars they bumped into, and Julienne was pleased more than one of them remembered her name.

She didn't feel so invisible beside Cece anymore. Not with the way Cece had whistled at her when she put the dress on, barely kept her hands to herself in the car over.

They stopped to talk to an interviewer, shadowed by a cameraman, and Julienne tried not to look as nervous as she felt. They hadn't done any prep for interviews, and Julienne was trying to get more comfortable with winging things.

Cece squeezed her hands.

The interviewer asked a few quick-fire questions about the show, about who Cece was hoping would win tonight, about what she was wearing. Then, finally, a question about Julienne:

"And who have you brought with you tonight?"

"This is my beautiful girlfriend, Julienne," Cece said. "It's her first red carpet, so be gentle."

Julienne's cheeks flushed as Cece shot her that trademark smirk.

"Well I hope you both have a great night, good luck," the interviewer said, and then they moved on. They separated, briefly, for Cece to give another interview, and Julienne was glad for the chance to get a breather.

She'd gotten a little more used to the click and flash of

cameras in the few months they'd been together – Sadie had insisted they alert the paparazzi for a few staged dates – but it still felt strange to be the focus of so much attention. Cece had always been right by her side though, willing to coach her through it, and Julienne loved her for that.

She couldn't help but feel proud of Cece as she watched her smoothly redirect the interviewer away from questions about her controversies on to something else. She was a natural.

The red carpet had to end eventually, and then they were given glasses of champagne and directed to their seats at a table full of people Julienne was far too starstruck to speak to. Cece gave her drink to Julienne, and Julienne sipped it slowly, trying to ignore the knots tying themselves in her stomach. Cece kept her arm loosely draped over Julienne's shoulder for the whole thing, and the scent of her perfume kept Julienne from feeling like she'd entered another dimension.

This was Cece's world, which meant Julienne had a place in it.

Julienne let herself be wrapped up in the glamour of the show for a few hours, until it was time for Cece's category to be called.

Julienne's chest felt tight as they read out the list of nominees for best supporting actress. They called Cece's name and Julienne smiled for the camera as they played a clip from Bare Windows. Once the cameras were off them she pressed a kiss to Cece's arm for good luck and sat up a little straighter. The category had some stiff competition, actresses with many years more experience than Cece, and Julienne almost couldn't believe that the woman she loved was up there with these huge names.

"...and the winner is..."

Julienne held her breath.

"Cece Browne, Bare Windows."

The applause started before the words had even sunk in, and soon the roar of it was deafening.

"Oh my god," Cece said, barely audible.

"I love you," Julienne said, as Cece pulled her into an embrace, pressed a kiss to her cheek. Her hands were shaking, and Julienne reached out to give one of them a quick squeeze. "You deserve this," she said.

Cece nodded, her eyes wide.

Julienne leaned in, pressed another quick kiss to her lips. "Go," she said, firmly.

Cece's face split into a grin, bright enough to take Julienne's breath away, and then she was gone, making her way up to the stage.

Julienne's heart was still racing and she was smiling so hard it hurt.

Her Cece, standing on stage, accepting an award.

She could already imagine the trophy beside that first one on the shelf, against that true blue wall.

Cece stepped up to the podium, and Julienne's breath caught in her throat.

Under all the bright lights, with the whole room's attention, Cece seemed to sparkle.

"I'm really proud of the work I've done on Bare Windows this season," Cece said. "I pushed myself harder than I ever have before."

She paused, looked for Julienne in the crowd.

Julienne was sure her smile could be seen from space.

"I obviously owe an incredible amount to Sam, the directors and writers, and the rest of the cast and crew. I'd also like to thank Sadie, for everything she's done, and Jules – she knows why. Most of all, I would like to dedicate this award to my mom, and I hope she'd be proud of the woman I am today."

Julienne's face was wet with tears as Cece disappeared backstage. An actor on her table gave her a sympathetic smile and passed a packet of tissues, and she took them with trembling hands.

Her makeup was definitely ruined, but she didn't care. It was worth it, to see Cece up there, proud of all her hard work. For every late night where Julienne had stayed up to run lines, every time Cece had called her to vent instead of arguing with the production team, all the weekends and parties Cece had missed. She'd put so many hours into making her performance the best it could be.

She dabbed at her face, then checked her makeup in her phone camera. Not flawless, but passable.

"You look gorgeous," Cece said, interrupting her.

"You are amazing," Julienne said.

Cece grinned. "I am kind of killing it right now, aren't I?"

Julienne couldn't help but smile back at her. Cece's joy, just like everything else, was magnetic, drawing Julienne in.

Cece moved her chair closer to Julienne's before she sat down, so their thighs were brushing against each other as they watched.

"I love you," Cece said.

Julienne pressed a kiss to the corner of her mouth.

Another category was announced and they went quiet to listen. Bare Windows wasn't up for this award, but there was still a nominee from Cece's circle of friends.

"You know," Cece said, her breath hot against Julienne's ears. "The only thing that would make tonight more perfect..."

She trailed off and Julienne's cheeks flushed pink. She

hoped Cece didn't mean anything that would cause headlines.

"What?" Julienne asked, nearly drowned out by the applause as the cameras cut to the various nominees.

"If there was an award here for you," Cece said.

"I don't think there's going to be a Best Receptionist award," Julienne said.

Cece shrugged. "I'll make one for you."

Julienne couldn't help but smile at that.

They quieted as the winner was announced, then politely applauded as the next winner was announced.

Cece's hand drifted to Julienne's knee, and the weight of it made Julienne feel like she was exactly where she was supposed to be.

Cece made her feel like she deserved the whole world.

Cece pressed a soft kiss to the side of her neck, and Julienne shivered.

"I love you," she said," but I have work tomorrow. You cannot give me a hickey."

Cece rolled her eyes. "Always assuming the worst," she said, still wearing a smile.

"I'm going for a promotion," Julienne said. "If I'm ever going to win any award I should keep things professional."

"Alright," Cece said. "We'll have to find a different way to celebrate, then."

Her hand drifted away from Julienne's knee and Julienne missed it immediately.

"You're the worst," she told Cece.

Cece grinned. "You love me."

"I do," Julienne said. "I'm so proud of you."

"I'm proud of me too," Cece said. "I'm proud of us."

Julienne couldn't wipe the smile off her face if she tried. They had a lot to be proud of.

NEWSLETTER

I'm an independent author, and reviews really help. If you enjoyed this book please rate and review!

Sign up for my newsletter at
https://bit.ly/3d1tpqR
to get a free bonus scene from Cece's POV and information about upcoming books!

ACKNOWLEDGMENTS

This book would not have been written without the support of WC, particularly Lou, Colin, Jason, Zoe, and Jake, who read and gave valuable feedback on various drafts of Love, Undisclosed, as well as J and Zoe (again) for insightful marketing advice. Thanks to Rena, for the cover design and also being very kind throughout the process, knowing it was my first novel. Thanks to Romance Writers Connect, for giving feedback on the blurb and answering all of my beginner marketing questions. Thanks to my family, for supporting me when I decided to take a break from jobhunting and try something different. There are many many friends who have offered support throughout the process, particularly EK, Imi, Devin, and many many others!

CPSIA information can be obtained
at www.ICGtesting.com
Printed in the USA
BVHW030502131021
618812BV00027B/206